I0573818

*Table of contents*

# The Almost-Widow

**The Borderline Chronicles, Volume 2.5**

Fiona West

Published by Tempest and Kite, 2019.

THE ALMOST-WIDOW

**First edition. October 4, 2019.**

Copyright © 2019 Fiona West.

ISBN: 978-1732877481

Written by Fiona West.

To my son and my daughter: may you always know that nothing holds you back from love but your willingness to give yourself, just as you are.

# Chapter One

SAM

"SIT DOWN, LIEUTENANT."

Sam Simonson sat down across from his commanding officer. The office was drab but orderly, much like the man who owned it. Colonel Pope folded his hands on the desk.

"First of all, we want to express our appreciation for your actions in the Heartwood Forest incident in Op'Ho'Lonia. You men spent a lot of time and effort looking for that traitor, Prince Lincoln, only to be attacked. You and Lieutenant Saint saved Lieutenant James's life. You're being awarded the king's medal for valor."

"Thank you, sir." Simonson knew this already; being friends with King Edward had its advantages. He'd been friends with Edward since officer's training school, back when he was second in line to the throne, a lowly prince. Saint had been friends with him back then as well, James even longer.

"But since your unit is going back into the reserves rather than active duty, we wanted to see if you'd be interested in a special assignment."

*Why am I being given a choice?*

"What kind of assignment, sir?"

"The king has requested you for his personal security staff. It seems that now he's a married man, he's a little more particular about who's standing outside his residence at night. But he made it clear that you should feel free to accept another assignment if you prefer." Sam was surprised that Edward hadn't said anything; he usually gave him a heads up about such things. Neither of them liked being put on the spot for a decision.

"What would that entail?"

"It's five twelve-hour shifts, 1700 to 0500 normally. You'd travel with His Majesty when necessary, but mostly, it's standing outside the residence with the grand duchess's security, Tezza Macias."

He remembered Macias. She was hard to forget, dressed head to toe in black, long black ponytail high on her head, toned stature. She was Op'Ho'Lonian; the winter weather had taken a toll on her skin tone, but it was decidedly more olive than the average light-skinned Orangiersian. The difference between the two would hardly be noticeable against his own dark skin, but it was there. The grand duchess, Abbie, had only had one close call with her opponents, and that wasn't on Macias's watch.

"Any idea why he asked for me specifically?"

Colonel Pope went on. "I believe His Majesty is concerned about the grand duchess's privacy as well as her safety . . . He expressed to me that he'd sleep better knowing there's someone highly dependable outside their quarters."

Sam nodded. He considered himself dependable as well, and he was flattered to know that Edward trusted him to keep him and Abbie safe. If that's what Edward needed, he'd be there for him.

"I'll do it."

"I'd also like to encourage you again to accept the promotion you've been offered, Lieutenant. There's no reason why you couldn't have your own command, especially now that you've got a commendation on your chest. It's the perfect time to think about moving up into your next role. You're a greater asset than you give yourself credit for."

"I'll think about it, sir."

The colonel's lips pressed into a line. "That's what you said last time, Simonson, but your letter of acceptance never crossed my desk." He gave him a pointed look over his reading glasses, and Sam looked away. He knew the colonel meant well, but he didn't know what to say. He was likely to have the same problem when drawn into conversation with Macias . . . He hoped she wasn't chatty.

The colonel sighed. "You start tomorrow night. Report at 1630 for orientation. Dismissed."

"Thank you, sir." He left quickly, though there was no reason to. He'd be up all night anyway, trying to get his body on the right schedule. Maybe he could get James to stay up with him; he was always up for late-night shenanigans.

## TEZZA

Tezza Macias set her groceries down on the counter of her bungalow and sighed. She'd gotten used to shopping late at night; after working the security night shift for months, that didn't bother her. Nor was she afraid to be out by herself. But the quiet in her house . . . that was something that still got under her skin, even now.

*Two years, 105 days.* Out of habit, she touched her husband's framed picture on the mantel as she searched for the remote to turn on the TV for background noise. The picture of her soldier used to live in her bedroom, but she'd relocated it to the mantel when she'd moved to Orangiers seven months ago to take this special assignment. She didn't know why. Grief was strange in that way; it never explained itself.

Magic gathered and pooled around her bare feet in a way that few could feel. Sighing, she flicked her wrist to turn on the TV with a small pop, and she felt the magic ripple with pleasure, warming her skin as it surged around her. All her usage lately had been purely utilitarian, as it was for most people inside the Veil. It wasn't that she couldn't do more, but lately, the drive just wasn't there.

*Where are you, Rocco?* Two years, 105 days ago, he'd called her to say he loved her just before he went incognito into a hostile area as a spy. According to the Op'Ho'Lonian Special Forces, they lost contact with him soon after that. She dropped to the floor and did some bicycle crunches, push-ups, stretched her back. It was more productive than crying. She'd fill her small house with the sound of exercise and television; it was better than letting the silence oppress her again.

They were showing more footage of her employer's wedding; she was amazed at this country's capacity for celebrity gossip. Then again, with Orangiers so meteorologically dreary this time of year, people did need something to keep them going, she supposed. King Edward, age twenty-two, had married his fiancée Abelia Porchenzii of Brevspor; they had been childhood friends, entering into an arranged marriage after signing a binding contract a decade before. It was a good match in many ways; both were a bit nerdy, bookish, intellectual, prone to banter and matching wits. Yet in Tezza's opinion, two stronger personalities had rarely been in the same room together, let alone shared a marriage. Abbie was now grand duchess rather than queen, due in part to a chronic illness that plagued her. Tezza didn't talk about that; silence was a virtue for a reason.

She'd been hired for her magical abilities; abilities that were now deteriorating from lack of use. As a non-tech magic user, she'd cultivated a relationship with the magic here in order to be able to protect the grand duchess during her engagement. Not everyone could feel the magic's pull, its vibrating tug on your body, but it had always been second nature to her. And here, inside the Veil, the magic had been tamed—groomed, really—to be more open to sharing itself. Most people took advantage of this by purchasing devices powered by magic: cell phones, fridges, stoves, etc. Even apart from the technology it powered, magic still required patience and the right words, but compared to the Unveiled, controlling it here was a cake walk. Tezza's abilities had been challenged just a few days before the royal wedding . . . but she'd protected the grand duchess when it counted. She'd take that secret to her grave; the spotlight held no attraction for her. Invisibility suited her best.

SAM

*JUST RELAX. IT'S A job. A job you know well. Edward asked you.* Sam stuck out his hand to the woman standing outside the palace security office.

"Good evening. We're assigned together, I believe. Sam Simonson."

She gave him a firm, businesslike handshake. "Tezza Macias. Nice to meet you."

"Same."

They stood in silence. His nervousness began to extricate itself from his chest.

"Ready to go up?"

"Yes."

They climbed the back staircase to the king's residence and got a status update from the previous guard: the royals were in for the night. The previous watch had no issues to speak of. They'd be relieved at 0500.

They took up posts on either side of the double doors. *Am I supposed to talk to her? I've never observed Dean and Waldo working. They probably talk.* He glanced over at the woman, but she didn't acknowledge him. *Good. That's fine, silence is good.*

At 2200, he heard a noise that sounded like breaking glass. He immediately got a text.

**Bluffton Security Central Dispatch: Outside sentries reported a crash inside the residence. Maintain radio silence.**

**Sam: Investigating now.**

He showed the screen to Macias, then pocketed his phone as he began to open the door to the residence.

"I can go," she said, putting a staying hand on his arm.

*That's uncomfortably familiar,* he thought. There was a scent clinging to her . . . a perfume or shampoo or something . . . *Plumeria. Gag.*

"I'm quieter," she asserted.

His eyes narrowed as he stared at the doors to the king's residence beyond her. "What makes you think that?"

"Watch." She started into the residence, and then she . . . faded. He didn't know how else to describe it. It was as if someone put a transparency filter on her. She turned to look at him, as if to say "Well?"

He nodded, then flicked his hand to say "Go for it." She disappeared around the corner, and a few minutes later she came back with a look on her face he couldn't interpret.

"Find anything?"

"It was nothing."

"It was nothing because you found nothing or because you know what the sound was?"

"The royals knocked over a lamp while having intercourse."

"Ah. I'll let Dispatch know." She didn't seem embarrassed by this in the least. In fact, though he struggled to read other people's nonverbals, if he had to guess, he'd say she was amused. He was also a little amused, but didn't let it show. *Professionalism and all that.* The night shift was bound to bring more intimate moments between them. The royals were lucky Arron James wasn't in his place or he'd be telling everyone within a five-mile radius.

She resumed her previous stance as he texted Central Dispatch back, giving them the all clear. He also let them know that the royals were awake and would likely be making more noise shortly. But in the back of his mind, the questions wouldn't leave him alone. He turned back to her.

"Did you speak with them?"

"No."

"Then how do you know they broke a lamp?"

"I could hear them laughing about it through the bedroom door, making bets on which of us was going to draw the short straw."

Sam grinned at his shoes; he was glad to hear they were laughing. Before Abbie, Edward didn't laugh enough. "Who guessed correctly?"

"She did. He thought you'd be more protective, more likely to burst through the door."

"A fair assessment." He wasn't embarrassed either. His friends had given him a hard time often enough about his naivety that it was no surprise Edward thought it would be him.

"Perhaps in part, but I'm very protective as well. She's a good person."

"They both are."

"Agreed."

They settled back into the silence, broken a few minutes later by two muffled, wordless cries from the residence, first hers, then his. Since Macias didn't react and he received no more text messages, he decided to follow Tezza's lead on this one. They didn't speak again until 0500 when their shift was over.

"Headed home?" He didn't know why he asked her that. It was probably intrusive.

"No." She shook her head. "I'm meeting my sister."

"Oh. Well, enjoy your time with her."

"Thanks. See you tomorrow."

"Yeah."

Edward was exiting the residence just as he started to walk away. "Hey, fancy a run?"

Sam shrugged. "Why not?"

"That's the spirit."

"How are you so chipper so early in the morning?" Sam asked.

"I have an exceptional constitution, mate, for I am an exceptional person."

Sam grinned. "Bollocks."

"Cuts me right to the heart, that does. How was your first night of work?"

"Fine."

Edward glanced at him. "Fine? Just . . . fine?"

Sam nodded.

"How's Macias to work with?"

"She seems very competent. Last night, I watched her fairly fade away when she went to check on . . . um . . ." He realized what he was saying too late and felt his face heat. Though they were both black, Sam envied Edward's darker complexion. He was sure Edward could tell he was blushing, given that he was grinning from ear to ear.

"Drat it all, Abbie was right. Don't tell her, all right?"

"Why, what'd you wager?"

"If she was right about who checked, there's a new horror movie she's going to make me watch. *What Lies Underfoot*, or something. She says my jumping and cringing is the best part." He gave an exaggerated shudder and Sam smiled at his shoes.

"Just let me change and I'll meet you outside."

"Sounds good."

Though they didn't usually talk much on their runs, Edward's confusion over his new bride's quirks seemed to give him plenty to discuss.

"She can't retire without doing the dishes," panted Edward. "Even if she's exhausted, falling-down tired. She'll stand there and wash them all up. You'd never know she'd been raised royal."

"I find that very practical," said Sam, wiping his brow with his sleeve. "The scent of dirty dishes alone can ruin my morning."

"You're a bit more sensitive than most in that, mate."

"True." That hadn't stopped his mother from expecting him to wash them. It wasn't like she had time, working with his father, and she believed making him do things that bothered him would be "good exposure therapy." She wasn't wrong, but that hadn't made it any less uncomfortable. Sam didn't usually mind that his family and friends were attuned to his sensory issues; for his last birthday, Edward had given him noise-cancelling headphones which were now part of his essential equipment. They understood how overstimulating it felt to look someone in the eye . . . at least, they understood in theory.

"What's the best part of being married?" Edward grinned and opened his mouth to answer when Sam cut him off. "Besides finally getting a leg over."

He feigned offense. "Is that any way to talk about my delicate grand duchess?"

Sam snorted. "I've heard her say worse."

"So have I. Just this morning, in fact, she rolled over and asked me to—"

Sam held up a hand. "Stop. It's bad enough I have to hear it through the door."

Edward turned them back toward Bluffton, on the path along the sea cliffs. "In all seriousness, the best part is living with my best friend. She knows it all; the good and the bad. She's always there for me. I love that."

Sam nodded. He would, too. But at this point in his life, it seemed about as possible as crossing the Orangiersian Ocean in a bathtub.

# Chapter Two

TEZZA

1930 HOURS. THREE DAYS since Simonson had joined her assignment. She couldn't quite figure him out. He wasn't overly talkative on duty, which she appreciated, but it was more than just the quiet. He hadn't flirted with her. She wasn't vain, but she knew she was prettier than average; and she seemed to attract more attention here, with her dark Op'Ho'Lonian hair and eyes. Yet he had made no attempt to size her up, from what she could tell. It was . . . surprising. Surprising, but not unwelcome, considering they both had a job to do that required total focus. Her own focus had drifted a bit more often since he'd started . . . Physically, he was just her type. Not ripped, just strong. He filled out the uniform nicely . . . It wasn't a crime to notice. She was married, not dead.

They hadn't been on duty long when Prince Simon approached the residence, his security, Kevin, trailing at a distance. It was unusual to see the nine-year-old apart from his mother or his nanny. It put her on high alert, even if it shouldn't. She was always more aware of Simon; not only did he stand out because he had trisomy 21, a genetic disorder that affected his development, but the magic loved him. She could barely get its attention when he was around.

"Hi, Simon," Sam greeted him. "What do you need, mate?"
"Uncle Sam, I need Eddie."

"This might not be a good time, Si . . ." She assumed Sam was referring to the knock-down, drag-out fight that was currently happening in the residence over the king's last-minute cancellation of a romantic getaway they'd planned. In her limited experience with them as a married couple, these fights often peaked into a shouting match, sometimes broken dishes, then devolved into stony silence, giving way a few hours later to boisterous makeup sex. Simple proximity to their emotional roller coaster was tiring, but she figured they had to find their equilibrium eventually. Hopefully.

"Can I give him a message for you?" Tezza offered.

"No. He said he'd read to me. I want him to come now." Though she showed no outward sign of being offended, he seemed to think better of his tone. "I want him to come now, *please*."

She checked her watch; Simon was probably on his way to bed. Not much time to wait. She was guessing the couple wouldn't want him listening in on their fight, anyway.

"What if I read to you?" Sam said, and Tezza glanced up, surprised. He either *really* did not want to bother the royals or he was kind of a nice guy.

Simon looked torn, then shrugged. "I have to sit on your lap."

"I have to stand on duty," said Sam. "How about if you just stand in front of me? I'll hold it like a teacher does, okay?"

"You could probably sit," Tezza murmured, but Sam shook his head.

He took the book from Simon and read the title aloud. "*The Sleepy Bulldozer*? Man, anything for a buck."

Tezza snickered, and she and Kevin shared a knowing look.

"What does that mean?" Simon asked.

"Nothing, mate." He cleared his throat. "'Bran the Bulldozer was a helpful little machine. He worked hard at the construction site all morning, pushing and pulling, digging and rigging.'" Sam flipped through the book in disgust. "You like this book, mate?"

Simon nodded. "Keep reading. Please."

"What does that even mean, rigging?"

"Mum didn't know."

"No, I expect not," Sam muttered, and Tezza pressed her lips together hard. "'After a busy morning of work, Bran was supposed to rest his tracks and hit the sack . . . but Bran didn't want to, so Bran ran.'"

The door behind them opened, and Simon's face lit up. "Eddie!" He ran to Edward and threw his arms around his older brother.

"I thought I heard you out here. Sorry, squirt, Abbie and I had to discuss something. Did Uncle Sam read your book already?"

"Only a bit. You do it better. He stops a lot."

"The book is complete nonsense," Sam grumbled, handing the book back to Simon, as he followed them down the hallway toward Simon's room. "Have you read this, Edward?"

"Yes," Edward chuckled, "many times. Why are you so incensed?"

"Because the boy should be reading classics, not this sh—"

"Language, Uncle Sam."

"Sorry."

The door behind her opened again, and Tezza turned to find Abbie, pillow under one arm, cell phone charger slung around the back of her neck, her backpack over the other shoulder, stuffed to the brim. Her thunderous expression efficiently conveyed that the "discussion" had not been over when Edward left. Tezza followed her as she stormed down the hall.

"May I help you carry something?" Tezza asked quietly.

"No," Abbie spat. "I've got it." She stopped in front of her old guest room, where she'd stayed on visits to Bluffton before the couple were married, her hand on the door. She sighed and turned to Tezza.

"You're married."

Tezza quirked an eyebrow. "Is that a question?"

"Did you ever fight like this?"

Tezza snorted in response, and Abbie smiled weakly. "Our first year of marriage. Our first trip staying with his parents. He sided with them on everything, all weekend. Never listened to my opinion at all, and I'd had it. His parents teased us later that they were surprised there was no blood on the walls when we emerged from the guest bedroom . . ."

"I guess everybody fights."

"Maybe," Tezza said, then looked into her charge's eyes. "What I found was more important was not whether we fought, but how we repaired the damage." She glanced toward the guest room door. "It's hard to make up when you're down the hall. Rocco felt it as disrespect, even if it was unintended."

Abbie nodded, sighing again. She rested her forehead against the guest room door. "This is hard."

Tezza nodded. "Marriage is hard. But you'll get it."

"Thanks, T."

"If we go back now, he won't know you left." Abbie glanced down the hall where Sam stood outside Simon's door, then nodded, quickly moving back toward the residence.

"I'm not having sex with him, though."

"That's not information I needed."

"Sorry," she chuckled. The door closed behind her, and Tezza could hear Abbie banging around in her kitchen.

Five minutes later, Edward and Sam came back down the hall. Neither acknowledged her, and Sam took up his place on the right side of the door again as it closed behind Edward.

"I'm curious," Simonson said, his velvet-smooth voice startling her. Orangies were always saying this; she'd learned that they were usually waiting for an invitation to ask a question, something no Op'Ho'Lonian would ever do.

"About?"

"About why you did that."

Tezza frowned. "Did what?"

"She was going to sleep in the guest room, but you stopped her."

"No, I didn't."

"Well, you said something that changed her mind . . ."

"We all need someone to tell us when we're screwing things up sometimes. She knows I'm married and asked for my opinion. I gave it."

He was silent long enough that she thought the conversation was over.

"I beg your pardon, but you're married?"

*Guano. I shouldn't have said that,* she thought, but she nodded in affirmation. Sharing that piece of information with new acquaintances usually prompted a lot more questions, and they still had the better part of the night to stand there together.

"Huh."

"Does that surprise you, Lieutenant?"

"Not at all, Macias. I just didn't realize . . . You don't wear a ring."

Tezza remembered vividly the day she'd taken off her ring. She wasn't giving up on Rocco—not at all. Never. It had killed her to take it off. But it was killing her more to leave it on, having a constant reminder of the suffering she carried around. It had ceased to be comforting to carry a piece of him . . . It had become a burden. She hated to think of him that way . . . and really, it wasn't him who was a burden, just his absence. And it wasn't something she could afford to be distracted by at work.

"Really, I'd have been more surprised if you weren't married, given your age and physical attractiveness."

*Is he hitting on me? For Woz's sake, I just said I was married . . .*

She tipped her head slowly to look at her new coworker. "My age?"

"Yes. You're over thirty, aren't you?"

*Beat around the bush, why don't you?* "Yes. I'm thirty."

"Well, I find that most people who reach that age have coupled in some way, which makes sense given that female fertility begins to decline slightly at that age." He continued to stare forward. "Do you have children?"

"No."

"Well, you might want to get on that, then, assuming you want them."

"Noted." She decided not to mention to this odd young man that her husband's absence made that impossible. She'd never wanted to parent alone, so they'd planned to start a family when he came back from this last mission. So much for that.

"Why don't you wear a ring? That's the social convention."

"It doesn't suit me," Tezza said, wishing he would drop it. She glanced over at Simonson again. He rarely looked at her; he'd barely even spoken to her beyond essential communication.

"I apologize. I don't excel at social cues and I have a hard time reading facial expressions, but your body language is indicating that I'm probably overstepping. Please feel free to just tell me so."

"Yes, you were overstepping." She paused. "But it's fine. You can just ask me what I'm thinking if you can't interpret my face. I don't mind."

"Really?" He didn't bother hiding his interest.

"Yes, really," she said, letting a little irritation leak into her voice. "I mean what I say."

"That's very helpful. Thank you. It's a liability in threat assessment, and I really would like to improve." He paused. "How can I help you improve?"

"What?" She tried to not to show her surprise . . . not that he was looking at her.

"I'd like to be mutually beneficial to each other. What are your weaknesses?"

This was an intimate conversation to be having with someone she barely knew. She valued directness, but this was a whole new level . . . but perhaps it was practical to go ahead and be up-front with each other.

"My magical connection isn't as strong as I'd like it to be; I've neglected it."

"How does one form a connection with magic?"

"Pay attention to it. Play with it. Just use it, really."

"Why haven't you used it?"

She sighed. "My husband went missing over two years ago."

"What does that have to do with using your magic?"

Tezza bristled. "I guess I just haven't felt like it since he disappeared."

"I see." Sam was quiet, and she could tell he was thinking by how he rubbed the edge of his shirt. "Is there a way I can help your depression?" *Depression*. She still didn't want to use the word; depression was for weak people. People who liked to talk about their feelings.

"I doubt it." The words came out vulnerable, and she felt the tears edging toward the surface. *Guano, pull it together, Macias.* She swept her gaze across the halls and corridors, trying to put her brain back in a working mode.

"Well, I'm game to try."

"Why?" *Woz.* Like it was just that simple. *Men.*

He shrugged one shoulder. "I like helping my friends."

"We're not friends, Simonson."

Her harsh tone didn't appear to bother him. "Fine. I like helping my *coworkers*."

When he turned, she could see how sincere he was. She tried to keep her doubt off her face. "Your offer is noted."

"What's that face mean?"

*I did promise to explain myself . . .* "I'm skeptical, but trying not to show it."

He turned back to the hallway. "I'll annihilate it."

She chuckled in spite of herself. "You'll annihilate my skepticism?"

"Yes."

"You sound determined."

"Indeed, I am. Prepare yourself."

Tezza said nothing, but smiled.

IT WAS 0300 ON A FRIDAY. Macias was antsy, swaying at her post. She was already thinking ahead to the afternoon—she'd promised to watch her nieces for her sister. Alba and Nic seemed to be struggling a bit lately, which was unusual for them. Very unusual. Since the rest of the family was back in Op'Ho'Lonia, she'd offered to do whatever she could to help, which in this case meant keeping the girls overnight so Alba and Nic could go to a bed-and-breakfast in Cobbleford. They were planning to leave this morning; since the girls would be in school on Friday, she could keep her schedule fairly normal. All she had to do was pick them up, feed them dinner and put them to bed. Saturday, she'd have to stay up past her normal "bedtime," but it was worth it.

It couldn't be that hard, right? There was always the park down the street or the children's museum if they got bored. Plus, she had playdough. She had movies. Movies were the answer to everything.

"So," Simonson said, sauntering over to her as if they were already in conversation, "I'm going to drop this radio, and you're going to catch it with magic."

"What?"

"One, two . . ."

Macias inwardly reached to rally the magic around her ankles, but it responded too slowly, sluggishly.

"Three." He dropped the radio. She reached out and caught it with her hand.

"Let's try again," he said, taking it back.

"Why?"

"You seem out of sorts. There's nothing happening, everyone's asleep. Come on. Let's use the time."

Tezza ignored her mild annoyance. "Fine. But hold it up higher, not at waist level."

He held it level with his head. "Better?"

She nodded and began to rally the magic, feelings its warmth start to flow like wax.

"Okay. One, two . . . three." He dropped it, but she still couldn't get it in time and it landed with a thump on the plush blue carpet. "Wait a moment. If this breaks, who's paying for it?"

"It's *your* radio."

"Mmm. Perhaps I should use something else," he said, picking up the radio, then straightening to dig through his pockets. "Here, let's use my keys." He paused, looking down the hall.

"See something?"

He kept staring, then shook his head. "Just a shadow. The keys?"

She nodded. "Yes. They're lighter, too."

"Sure. Ready?"

She nodded again, and she actually felt a bit excited. He held them at waist level again, and she reached out and lifted his elbow with one finger until it was at eye level, only to find him actually looking at her. Sam grinned and she worked to keep a straight face.

"Stop smiling."

"Why? I enjoy seeing you squirm a bit. You've got everyone around here terrified, you know."

She lifted an eyebrow. "Even you?"

Still grinning, he dropped the keys without warning. She threw out a mattress spell, and they ricocheted off the magic buffer two inches from the ground with a pop. She caught them on the bounce.

"That's cheating, Macias. I said to catch them."

She held them out with two fingers, feeling smug. "And I did."

He took them from her, frowning. "Yeah, after you bought yourself more time. Catch it *in the air* this time."

Once she'd mastered catching them before they hit the ground, he tossed them up in the air and had her catch them at the top of their ascent. The magic was humming, pleased. He threw them at her chest, and they only got through her barrier twice; his arm was surprisingly strong. She was smiling and sweating lightly by 0500 and a bit more sorry than usual to say goodbye to her coworker.

# Chapter Three

SAM

A FEW DAYS LATER, SAM was still asleep when Tezza texted him.

**Macias: I need help. Come over.**

**Simonson: What's wrong?**

**Macias: You won't be late to work. 237 Terrence Terrace, East Cheekton.**

**Macias: Hurry.**

**Simonson: Is everything okay?**

**Simonson: Hello?**

233, 235, 237 Terrence Terrace. He looked up at the small bungalow. He looked down at his phone again. This couldn't be right. The mosaic-tiled house number in bright primary colors seemed so at odds with Macias's clothing style: all black, all the time. He'd literally never seen her wear another color. He headed up the walkway lined with winter-blooming camellias—she gardened? Really?—and knocked on the red front door. It was thrown open a moment later.

"Finally. What took you so long?"

*That's not exactly a greeting, but . . . okay.* "I'm here now, grumpy trousers. What's wrong?"

"I'll tell you what," she fumed. "The last person who owned this house was a chauvinist pig."

He followed her into the house, stopping short at the sight of the bathroom.

"What the . . ."

"Like I said." The bathroom was flooding . . . sort of. It was clear that the toilet had overflowed. She'd spelled the door so that everything was contained to the bathroom, but it was stacking up anyway, spilling over into the tub and down the drain.

"Wow."

"Yeah. I need you to go turn off the water to the toilet underneath so that it stops overflowing. That idiot spelled it so that only a man or a plumber could turn it off. Probably to make himself indispensable to his woman, to make up for what I assume were serious shortcomings in the bedroom."

Sam bit his cheek so he wouldn't laugh. He'd heard of magically inclined men using similar tactics so that their wives didn't mess with the electrical systems or zap themselves with temperamental appliances. She seemed so genuinely perturbed by this.

"Why didn't you turn it off outside at the meter?"

"I don't know how to do that!" she yelled, throwing her hands in the air.

"All right, all right," he soothed, "but you owe me."

"Fine."

He took off his socks and shoes, preparing to wade into the knee-high water. "Wait, aren't my pants going to get wet?"

"So take them off."

Embarrassment prickled along the back of his neck. "I'm not doing that."

She rolled her eyes. "Woz, Orangies are such prudes. Fine, I'll turn my back." Arms crossed, she spun around, her high ponytail whipping him in the face.

"You owe me big, Macias."

"Fine, fine. Just do it."

Sam dropped his pants and tossed them over the door in case things with her containment went sideways. At least he was wearing boxers today. He didn't think they had any holes in them. "Do you need to reinforce your barrier before I cross it?"

"My barrier is fine, thank you," she huffed.

"No need to take it personally . . ."

He felt a tingle as he passed through her invisible dam in the doorway, then slogged his way over to the toilet and turned off the water. Hearing his success, she popped her head in the door. "I'm going to pass you a bucket. Can you start to bail it into the tub?"

He put his hand on his hips. "Hey! What happened to privacy?"

"You look like a man," she drawled. "Big surprise."

"Don't make me spell the toilet so only men can *use* it."

She threw back her head and laughed, and he caught the bucket she tossed at his head. He carefully scooped water into the tub, trying not to get it on his hands.

"How dirty is this water, anyway?"

"My niece sent her Jungle Jane action figure down the 'sinkhole' yesterday, apparently. It's mostly clean, petunia."

"I'm not sure I care for that nickname . . . Woz, this water is cold. Say, why aren't you in here?"

"I'm coming," she called, and a moment later, Tezza crossed the barrier wearing neon-pink workout shorts that barely covered her backside and a tight black spandex workout shirt. Sam really wished he wasn't standing next to her with only a thin layer of cotton between them. *Think about unsexy things. Lady-bugs. Baby food. Taxes. Spelling bees.*

"You're slowing down. Move it." She stuck her hand into the toilet and came out with the offending toy, which she dumped into the trash can. After ten minutes' work, the standing water was down to an inch. "Okay, that's good. Stand back."

He exited the bathroom, but stayed near the door to watch her work; he hadn't gotten to see her practice since the night he'd made her catch his keys. She didn't bother whispering since it was just the two of them. She wove her spell, a gathering incantation for scattered items, carefully twirling her finger in a circle, pulling the water up into a tornado-like shape before depositing it into the tub. She seemed to be good at repurposing incantations, reinventing them.

"Nice."

"Thanks. Pass me the mop, will you? There's still a few puddles."

"I can do it. You go get dressed for work."

"Are you sure?"

"Positive. Go. You've clearly been dealing with this all afternoon. I just got here. You must be tired, you don't need to add mopping as well." He shooed her out of the bathroom, before putting his pants back on and getting to work sanitizing all non-porous surfaces and wiping up trace amounts of water.

She soon strolled back in, wearing her typical head-to-toe black. "So since I owe you 'big,' your words, can I buy you breakfast?"

He shrugged as he retrieved his backpack. "Sure. I thought I was the only one who still called it breakfast on the night shift."

"What else would you call it?"

"Well, traditionally, the third meal of the day is called dinner or supper, depending on where you're from."

"But it isn't *my* third meal of the day."

"Precisely my thinking. I'm glad I'm not alone."

She gifted him with a small smile. "So am I."

He pointed at her. "But do you still eat breakfast food?"

"Of course. And I know a place that does a fabulous Op'Ho'Lonian omelet. Since I'm a regular, they'll still make it for me in the afternoon. They make their own sour cream and salsa."

Sam wrinkled his nose as he helped her into her coat. "I don't know that I care for salsa on my eggs . . ."

Tezza patted his shoulder patronizingly. "I have so much to teach you."

"WELL?" TEZZA WATCHED him expectantly as he tasted his first bite of the omelet. Salty, soft cheese met his tongue with the acid of the lime and tomato in the salsa. The cilantro was . . . strong.

"It's a bit herby, but it's good." He added a little more sour cream and took a second bite. "It's good. I'll eat it."

"How generous of you," Tezza deadpanned, and he chuckled.

"I never had this when I was in Op'Ho'Lonia."

"Why were you there?"

"Hunting for Lincoln." Her face changed. *Her eyebrows just went up, her mouth opened a little.* "What's that face?"

She blinked at him. "I'm surprised, I guess. I didn't realize you were involved in the search for the traitor. You don't seem like the type to request that kind of assignment."

He shrugged one shoulder. "It needed to be done. James and Saint wanted to go. They wanted me along. I'm better at tracking than they are."

"They said you saved Arron's life."

Sam stared down at his plate, pushing the melting cheese back from the potatoes. "He'd have been fine whoever had been there. He's recovering well." He didn't like talking about Op'Ho'Lonia. He'd gotten too much attention for it already.

"The grand duchess was very upset when it happened."

"Was she? Why?" He took a bite, chewing slowly. "She hadn't met any of us yet."

Tezza sipped her coffee, gripping the mug. "But she wanted to, because you're important to him." Sam liked Abbie. She was pretty easy to talk to, though she did like to tease him. But the rest of his friends did, too; he was an easy target, he knew. They meant no harm.

She went on. "She also lost her sisters at a young age unexpectedly. That leaves a mark on a person."

"Indeed it would."

"Are your parents alive, Simonson?"

He nodded. "They live in Saffolk. He's a lawyer. She's a mum, but she helps with the accounting."

"Do you have brothers and sisters?"

He shook his head. "Just one strange whelp for my poor parents."

"Don't say that." There was scorn in her tone.

"Why?" he asked lightly, stabbing a potato. "It's true. You've got a sister, haven't you?"

Her eyes narrowed, but she let him change the subject. "One sister, Alba, living here with her husband, Nic. Four brothers, still in Op'."

"And where do you fall in order? No," he interrupted himself, "let me guess . . ." He pointed his fork at her. "You're the baby."

"Yes."

He grinned. "I knew it. You don't give a burnt brownie what anyone thinks. That smacks of a child that knows it's beloved. And you fight like a child left to its own devices."

She pushed her plate away, despite having half an omelet left. "Whereas you act like an only child who had no one tell him to be quiet."

He tried to keep a straight face. "That's hurtful."

She tilted her head to give him a side-eye stare. "No, it's not."

Sam chuckled, dragging her abandoned plate over to his side of the table. "You're right, it's not. Though I rarely get told to be quiet. Mostly to speak up." He glanced up at her. "You seem to bring out the talker in me." *Which is strange, now that I think about it . . .*

The waiter stopped by the table, leaving the bill in front of Sam. Tezza quickly reached out and pulled it toward her.

"Woz, I didn't know you were going to break the bank when I offered to pay for breakfast."

"You don't have to pay for my breakfast, Macias. I've got it."

"I'm kidding, I'll pay."

"I'm not. I have very few expenses. I'm happy to help you . . ." He swallowed. "Anytime. You needn't feel obligated."

"I do what I say I'll do. You can pay next time."

*Next time? Oh. Next time. Didn't know we were having a next time . . .* He felt his face flush, then chided himself for being so easily embarrassed. He knew he should say something, but he wasn't sure what . . .

"Okay, but I get the pick the location, then."

"Fine," she said, pulling out a slim wallet from her backpack.

"And there'll be no cilantro on the eggs, I can promise you that."

She threw her napkin at him, and he dodged it, chuckling.

# Chapter Four

SAM

SAM WAS IN A GOOD MOOD when he arrived at work a few days after their breakfast outing.

"All right?" Saint was leaning against his locker, arms folded.

"All right," Sam answered, waiting for him to move. "What're you doing here?"

"Heard something. Something you need to hear."

"What's that?"

"Rumors about you and Macias."

Sam looked into Saint's face. He didn't do it often; despite being friends for years, he found the man intimidating, and besides, looking at him was seldom useful, as Saint's face rarely gave away what he was thinking. *Closed expression, mouth tight, brows drawn together. Concern.*

"What kind of rumors?"

"Someone saw you leaving her house together. Someone else saw you at a café, laughing, having dinner together."

"She needed help with a house problem. I helped her, and she paid me in breakfast."

"You mean dinner."

"No, I mean breakfast; the first meal of *my day* is called breakfast."

"You're getting distracted again. Listen to what I'm saying: they found it suspicious."

Sam's gaze narrowed. "Suspicious how? She's married."

"Exactly, Sam. She's married, but her husband is missing. You were alone together in her house, and then you went on a date."

"It wasn't a date!" he shouted, and Saint held up a quelling hand, glancing around the locker room. "*She paid*, for Woz's sake!"

"I'm not saying it was, mate. But they're saying there's something going on between you."

Cold fury surged in Sam's heart. "So you're saying that I've actually made a female friend for the first time ever, and now everyone thinks I'm getting a leg over on a married woman? Fantastic. That figures. Thanks for the heads up. I need to get into my locker."

"Calm down, mate."

"Too jacking late."

Saint stepped back. "You just need to be aware of how it looks to others, all right? I know you, you mean well, but you don't realize. You don't want to damage her reputation."

This gave him pause. *That's true, I don't want her to suffer because of me.*

He took a deep breath and let it out slowly as he put his backpack away. "Thank you for letting me know."

Saint gave him a quick nod, put on his aviator sunglasses, then left.

HE TRIED TO SHAKE OFF the feeling of guilt as he walked toward the residence. Sam wished he could keep walking, take a few laps around the palace before starting work, but Tezza was already there, and he didn't want to keep Dean waiting. They nodded their greetings. Around 2200 hours, she broke the silence.

"Heard some yelling from the men's locker room earlier," Tezza said.

He grunted.

"It sounded like you."

"It was me." He took a deep breath and let it out slowly; his neck and shoulders still felt locked up just thinking about it. "I hate everyone."

"Everyone?" *What was that tone in her voice? Oh . . .*

"I guess there's a scant few whom I don't hate. But the list is short, I tell you. Short. And today, it got shorter still."

"My mom says if everyone's an idiot, you're stressed."

He snickered. "Your mum is wise."

"Yes." She paused. "What were you yelling about?"

"Doesn't matter."

"If you say so, Simonson."

Out of the corner of his eye, Sam saw something move, but when he turned his head, there was nothing there. It almost looked like . . . but it couldn't be.

"What is it?"

"Thought I saw something, but my eyes must be playing tricks on me . . ."

"Same thing you saw the other night?"

He nodded.

"Doesn't hurt to check," she said. "You go. You know what you saw."

Sam stalked down the hall toward the music conservatory. He peered into the room with one hand on his knife, then stepped inside. There was a grand piano on the far side of the room, and the moonlight streamed in through a large picture window. Most of the other instruments were put away in cupboards, and the padded chairs for the seating area were stacked neatly in the corner. He walked around the piano, even looked underneath. There were few places for a cat to hide in here. Sam opened one of the cupboards that was slightly ajar, but all he saw were violins, stacked in black cases. He shook his cell phone flashlight on, shone it deeper into the space. Nothing. And the rest were closed tight, as were the windows.

Shaking his head, he strode back to the residence.

"Central Dispatch," he spoke into the radio.

"Go ahead, Kingsguard One."

"Did the royals get a cat or anything I don't know about?"

"Cat?" He heard the man mutter something he couldn't understand. "I'll ask."

He arrived next to Macias and shook his head.

"Kingsguard One?"

"Go ahead," Sam replied into the radio.

"No cat. The queen mother's allergic."

"Copy."

Macias turned her head. "You thought you saw a cat?"

"I know I did. Tortoiseshell, sleek. Orange and black with a white chest." He patted his own chest for emphasis, then shook his head again. "I must be losing my mind."

"Perhaps not. It could be a magical apparition. But it takes a powerful user to conjure something physical from a distance . . ." She turned to look down the hall. "Would you mind if I tried to feel the magic in there? If it's focused on someone else, I may be able to tell."

"No, go right ahead," he said, waving toward the conservatory. She broke off at a jog and he watched her go, shaking his head. He hadn't expected her to believe him at all, let alone take measures to confirm his suspicions. It was just a cat . . . but what if it was gathering information for someone about the royals? What if it got into their quarters somehow? Edward's brother, Lincoln, was still at large; he'd betrayed the family several times already. Something like this was not beneath him. He and his fiancée had launched some kind of attack at Abbie and Edward's engagement masquerade; that information was classified, but he'd heard a few of the details secondhand. And what he'd heard was enough.

Sam shuddered and steeled his resolve. Nothing was going to get past him. Not tonight.

WOMEN HAD BEEN SMILING at him all day. Sam couldn't figure it out. Was it the uniform? He was given to understand that women liked uniforms, though he couldn't fathom why. It seemed so shallow to him to be interested in someone based solely on clothing that hundreds of other men also wore.

Maybe they weren't smiling in attraction. Maybe they were amused . . . Had he put something on inside out? Before leaving the grocery store, he checked his reflection in the big windows out front. Everything seemed fine. It was truly perplexing. It was still nagging at him as they stood outside the residence at 2100 hours.

"So, as a woman . . ." Sam caught himself. That was an inappropriate question. "Never mind."

"I hate that phrase."

"Which one? 'As a woman'?"

"No. 'Never mind.'"

"Really?"

She nodded. "Rocco and I have a deal where if one of us says 'never mind,' they have to do one hundred push-ups."

"That seems a bit harsh," he mused. "Why do you hate it so much?"

"Because I'm curious now, Simonson. I hate being left in suspense. You started the sentence, just finish it."

"I don't want to be invasive."

"I'm used to it by now."

He gave her half a smile. "As a woman, does anything look different about me today?" He turned toward her so she could see him better and held out his arms like he was being searched at the airfield.

"No. Why?"

"Women have been *smiling* at me."

"So?"

"So they don't usually notice me at all. It's odd. I'm wondering what the contributing factors are."

She scoffed. "Why?"

He scowled. "I simply don't care for undue attention from strangers."

"You're so—" She stopped.

He lifted an eyebrow. "I'm so ... what?"

"Nothing," she muttered.

"No, that's the same as 'never mind.' You owe me one hundred push-ups."

"Fine. But only because I can use the exercise." She handed him her radio and started. "You have to count," she grunted.

"Oh, sorry. What's the count, then?"

"Ten."

He continued on from there and was up to fifty-six when the residence door opened.

"Grand Duchess." *Fifty-seven, fifty-eight, fifty-nine . . .*

Abbie smiled. "Tezza. Sam. You look nice today, Sam."

"Really?" He forgot all about counting for Tezza. "By what measure?"

Both women chuckled. "Just take the compliment," Abbie chided gently. "Tezza, doesn't Sam look nice today?"

"Yes." She popped up, abandoning their agreement. "What can I do for you, ma'am?"

"Parker and I want to go for a horseback ride in the snow."

"It's snowing?" Sam tried to peer out the French doors at the end of the hall, but it was too far to see.

She nodded. "Can you make the arrangements?"

"Certainly." Tezza gave a curt nod, and Abbie smiled as she went back into the residence. "Radio."

He handed it back to her, and she radioed down to the stables. Sam got his own radio out and called up alternates so they could go to the locker room and get warmer clothes. Within twenty minutes, they were starting their ride through the woods.

"You want point?" he asked.

She nodded, taking the lead. The truth was that he wanted to be able to see all of them. He preferred the back. Less pressure. Not that he was expecting anything to happen in the patrolled, private woods around Bluffton at 2130 hours. They chose a wide path so Edward and Abbie could ride side by side. The royals were unexpectedly quiet. Maybe it was the snow; it wasn't deep, just a dusting that would probably be gone by morning, but it was muting the horses' footfalls, and the air made him just want to breathe in deep and smell the pine and the cold.

Sam was distracted. Why had Tezza said there was nothing remarkable about his appearance, and then agreed with Abbie that he looked nice? He stared at her profile; she always looked nice. Being on the wide path meant there was more light from the clouds reflecting off the snow. Tezza had floated some kind of spelled light out in front, and the contrast was making her dark features even more stunning than usual. He pulled out his phone to ask her about their conversation earlier, then thought better of distracting her. But he couldn't resist taking just one picture of her when she looked like that. *I'll delete it later,* he promised himself, and he popped the reins to catch up.

He didn't turn his head soon enough to get a good look at the tortoiseshell cat that climbed a leafless tree and disappeared into the dark of the forest canopy, but the sinking feeling in his gut told him that its presence here probably wasn't a coincidence.

# Chapter Five

### SAM

HE FOUND OUT WHY STRANGE women were smiling at him when, the next day, he saw an announcement on the news about the medal he was getting for the Op'Ho'Lonian mission. They'd used a picture of him, Saint, and Arron sitting on a fallen log over a raging river . . . They'd sent that picture to Edward. It bothered Sam that a token of friendship was now being used to embarrass him. But really, the whole mission had been a token of friendship.

Tezza waited until 0210 to bring it up.

"Were you going to invite me?"

He tried to play dumb. "To what?" *Please be talking about something else . . .*

"Your medal ceremony. It's tomorrow night. They asked me if I wanted a replacement."

"Don't."

"Don't what?"

"Don't get a replacement. Abbie should have a quiet night in."

She widened her stance a little. "My understanding is that they're both attending."

Sam cursed. "Why, why would she do that?"

"Keep your voice down. Why wouldn't she? You're friends."

"Of course we're friends. But she doesn't like going out at night. She shouldn't have to."

He could hear the smirk in her voice. "So you can sacrifice for them, but no one can sacrifice for you?"

*Yes. Exactly.* He couldn't stand still. He paced ten steps down the hall, then paced back. Out and back, out and back.

"It's not just about you. Saint and James are getting theirs, too."

He plucked at his bottom lip. "That's true."

"So back to my original question . . . were you going to invite me?"

"No, I wasn't." He took up his place by the door again, adjusting his radio. "I didn't invite my parents, either, but they're coming anyway."

"Okay."

Something in her voice made him glance over at her. *Body pointed away, posture rigid, eyes downcast.* "I'm sorry, did you want to come?"

She shrugged. "Not if you don't want me there."

"Macias . . ." He sighed. "Fine. You can come. Everyone else in the universe is."

She squared her posture and smiled. "Simonson, most people crave public gratitude. If we don't honor soldiers, we won't have enough of them. Consider the greater good."

He paused. "Thank you, Macias, that's a good point. I will . . . try."

"Good."

TEZZA

ACCUSTOMED AS SHE WAS to having military men in her life, even Tezza had to admit that Sam looked hot in his dress whites. Uncomfortable, but hot. She was guessing the discomfort had more to do with being in the spotlight than being in a stuffy uniform. Funny how the moment she made it sound like he was doing them all a favor by accepting a medal, his shoulders had dropped and he'd started breathing normally again.

She was regretting not working the event, however. Her substitute on Abbie's detail was standing much too far away from her; she wasn't even doing a proper sweep—she'd had her back to her protectee for five minutes solid. *Maybe I should just scoot down closer* . . . Before she could get up, they dimmed the house lights, and everyone applauded as Edward was announced and took the stage.

"Tonight," he said, "I have the illustrious pleasure of awarding medals to three men I've known for many years. I know two of them have a lot of celebrating to do tonight"—he glanced at them askance as the auditorium chuckled—"so I'll attempt to keep this brief." *He knows Sam well, apparently.* Edward's speech was the usual political rhetoric about duty and country and bravery, so Tezza tuned him out. Sam was looking off toward the doors longingly, his leg bouncing. He was in the second row on the end, but she knew he couldn't see her because of the lights in his face. She couldn't stand seeing him so anxious. An idea came to her. *What could it hurt?* She pulled out her phone.

**Macias: Your zipper's down.**

She almost gave in to a giggle as he pulled out his phone and read her message, horror etched on his face giving way to amused irritation.

**Simonson: Couldn't be. I checked.**

**Macias: For the greater good . . .**

**Macias: Try to look like you actually care.**

**Simonson: I do care.**

**Macias: Tell your face.**

**Simonson: I knew I shouldn't have invited you.**

**Macias: Rude.**

**Simonson: Troublemaker.**

His grin gave her a strange feeling in her chest that she ascribed to patriotism and camaraderie and courage. He turned toward Edward and appeared to listen attentively the rest of the evening, even managing to flash the crowd a smile when the king pinned the medal on his chest. Tezza slipped out as soon as the ceremony was finished . . . pausing only to text Abbie's replacement security that she'd be taking over the rest of the night.

SAM

THREE DAYS LATER, PRECISELY at 1500, Sam arrived at the Frothingham Café in West Cheekton. It was halfway between her house and the palace, appropriately public, not romantic, not too loud. A good number of young men with unnecessary glasses and buns hung out there, so he thought that would amuse her. He'd thought more about what Saint had said, and he certainly didn't want to stir up gossip. But perhaps if people saw them together often, they would understand that they were just friends. *Just friends.*

He ordered a tall Trellan deep roast and found a table away from the door which would not be drafty. At 1505, he texted her: **On your way?** He debated whether or not to start on his coffee, which was getting cold. At 1510, he took a sip of his coffee and tried again: **Stuck in traffic? Can't find it? Abducted by pirates?**

At 1517, he got up and left. He couldn't imagine that she'd forgotten. Would a friend go by her house and check on her, or was that too possessive? One of their nosy coworkers would perhaps see him if he went there again . . . but what if something was wrong? A friend, surely, could walk by her house and see if the lights were on. And since they were, at 1545, Sam knocked on Tezza's red front door.

No one answered. He texted her one more time: **You home?**

When he received no answer, he knocked louder. He cupped his hands around his face to peer in the narrow window beside her front door and saw her lying on the floor. "Macias!" he yelled. Frantic, he tried the knob and it opened. When the door hit the wall, she sat up, startled. "Are you okay? What happened?" He knelt on the floor next to her, leaving the door wide open.

"I was dusting," she hiccupped, "and the feathers caught in the edge of the frame, and it fell . . ." She held out the broken picture of a dark-haired man in an Op'Ho'Lonian Special Forces uniform she'd been holding to her chest. He took it from her and pulled her into his arms as her sobs started afresh. Relief flooded through him.

"Shh," he said, pressing her head to his shoulder. "It's okay, Macias. It's going to be okay," he murmured. He tugged on her ponytail. "We'll get a new frame."

"What are you doing here?" she forced out past her sobs.

"Coffee, remember? When you didn't respond to my messages, I became concerned."

"I'm s-sorry," she said, shaking her head.

"For what?" he asked, baffled.

"Making you wait. Being dramatic, being a mess."

He squeezed her lightly. "Stop. You broke an object that means something to you. Of course you're sad about that. I'd be more worried if you weren't sad about it."

"I'm tired of being sad," she choked out.

"I know." He squeezed her tighter and let his chin rest on top of her head.

"Hello?" A woman who looked a little like Tezza, except shorter and heavier with a pleasant round face, stood in the open doorway. "Everything okay in here?"

"Come in," Tezza said, shifting quickly out of Sam's embrace, wiping her tears. He'd held her without thinking about it, and the woman's quizzical look shamed him. "I broke Rocco's picture."

"Oh," the woman murmured, her eyes sad. "That's upsetting."

The woman knelt with them on the ground, crossing her ankles under her despite the broken glass, and began to rub Tezza's back. After a moment, to his shock, Tezza leaned back onto his shoulder as the woman continued her backrub.

"I'm Sam," he said, offering his left hand, since his right was pinned by Tezza's awkward lean.

"Alba," she replied, giving his hand a squeeze. Tezza sniffled, wiping her nose on her sleeve.

"The sister?" he asked, and she nodded.

"You must be the coworker."

He nodded back. "Coworker and occasional comforter in trying times."

"I see that. Friendship, we call it."

"Female friendship is new for me. It has many pitfalls." He chided himself for being too candid, but Alba smiled. *The smile reached her eyes, so that's genuine. No tension in her neck or face.*

"Looks to me like you're doing fine," she said softly. Tezza sat up slowly, wiping her face again, and Sam noticed a dark smear on her tawny cheek. He yanked her hand toward him.

"You're hurt!" He gently wiped the blood off her index finger with the edge of his shirt to try to discern how deep it was, and she hissed and pulled back. "You might need stitches."

"There's a first aid kit under the kitchen sink." Alba started to get up, but he signaled for her to stay and rose quickly to get it.

"That's not a good place for it," he said. "It could be damaged during a flood or a plumbing incident."

"Where would you keep it?"

"The kitchen is fine, but it should be higher, certainly out of the reach of children."

"I don't have any children, petunia."

"Stop calling me that," he said. Inwardly, he was glad she was teasing him again, because she seemed to be recovering a little from what seemed to be quite the traumatic event. His heart went out to her; he couldn't imagine how hard it must be to lose your spouse, even temporarily. He knelt next to her and pulled her hand toward him, less gruffly this time, adding some teasing of his own. "I did some research, and petunias are actually quite hardy. So it's not even a proper insult."

"Who said it was an insult?" she asked. He opened an alcohol wipe packet with his teeth and swabbed her cut.

"That hurts." She tried to pull back, but he held her wrist.

"Tough."

Alba smirked and with a slap of her thighs, she got to her feet. "Well, you seem to have things in hand, so I'm off. I was just coming by to drop off those herbs." She kissed the top of Tezza's head, then paused in the doorway. "Sam, it was so nice to meet you."

"Likewise," he said, not taking his eyes off his work of cleaning the blood from Tezza's finger, and he heard her shut the door quietly.

"Simonson." She tried to pull her hand away.

"What?"

"I can do this myself."

He scoffed. "One-handed? Better than I can? I don't think so." In his peripheral vision, he saw her lips purse, and he wasn't sure if she was annoyed or holding back a smile. "I've got this," he said as he gently pinched the wound shut and dabbed liquid adhesive on it in lieu of stitches.

"I see that."

"You're not arguing with me. And that's a command, not an observation."

"Who, me? No, I'm not arguing with you. I wouldn't dare."

He chose a bandage suitable for fingers and ripped off the outer layer.

"Do I really need both?"

"Quiet." He blew on her finger to dry the adhesive faster. She shivered. "Are you cold? I don't think you could have a fever from an infection so quickly. That's rather odd, really, I—"

"Yes, I'm . . . I'm cold."

For a long moment, he considered what had just happened. Her tone was off, stilted. But he was too distracted to figure it out, so he let it slide. "Right. I'm almost done. Then I'll get you a sweater."

"I don't want a sweater," she muttered, turning her face away from him.

TEZZA

He'd held her, really held her. Woz, how she'd needed it. She'd drunk it deep, greedily; just his steady presence was like brandy, warming her up. She felt embarrassed now that she'd gone back to him when she could've easily gone to Alba for comfort, but she hadn't wanted Alba. She'd depended too much on her these last few years.

She'd wanted Sam. If she was crying, he'd comfort her, he'd let her get closer. She didn't know if he'd felt manipulated; he'd tensed when Alba arrived, probably concerned with appearances. He had no idea, of course, that Alba thought she'd waited too long for Rocco and would be thrilled to see her getting attached to someone else. Her sister had pressured her at the turn of the year to have Rocco declared dead until Tezza finally told her to back off. It wasn't that simple. Alba meant well, but she didn't understand what it was like. There was no evidence he was dead. There was no evidence that he wasn't, Alba had argued back. But that wasn't enough, not for the man she loved wholeheartedly. It wasn't enough to say we couldn't know one way or the other. She needed to know. She needed to know for sure that he'd never show up on her doorstep with his black duffel again.

The only thing that gave her pause was the conversation she'd had with Rocco before he left on his first deployment. They'd made love over and over that night until they were both exhausted. She wanted to let him fall asleep first, to make sure they were done, but her eyes were so heavy . . . He'd pulled her close, whispered, "If something happens to me, I want you to remarry."

"Don't say that."

"I'm serious, babe. There's no such thing as a soul mate. If I'm gone, I want you to find somebody who makes you happy. Maybe not too handsome, but good for you." She'd grinned at that, nuzzling him with her nose.

"You'll come back."

"Of course I will. But if I don't . . ."

"You will," she'd said, taking his face in her hands, kissing him so he'd be quiet . . . but then they were off and running again, the pajamas she'd just put on being pulled off once more.

# Chapter Six

SAM

FORSYTHIA'S ENGAGEMENT ball was in full swing. Sam and Tezza had been assigned door duty for the main ballroom entrance. That suited him just fine; it was hard enough to deal with the noise when he was just standing outside the door. He patted down the men for weapons, confirmed IDs for the palace staff if he didn't know them already. By 2200, there wasn't much activity for them to deal with; everyone was inside having fun—if you could call being in close quarters with a bunch of overly fragrant, sweaty men and women "fun."

Macias was unusually chatty.

"Favorite movie."

He pulled his lips to one side. "You'll laugh."

"I won't."

"*A Prince in Disguise*."

She laughed. "A chick flick. Of course, petunia."

He wrinkled his nose at the moniker. "What's yours?"

"*Ten Days in Jersey*."

"A war movie, of course. I'd expect no less from you."

"You're a soldier, you should get it."

"I'm a soldier by default."

"So you joined the military because your friends did?"

"More or less."

"Huh."

He scanned the hallway. "What does that mean, Macias?"

"It just doesn't seem like a natural fit."

Sam bristled. "What does *that* mean, Macias?"

Their conversation was put on pause as Prince Simon, his mother, Lily, and their security passed by, presumably on their way to put him to bed.

"You're just . . . you're Simonson," Tezza continued. "You're a feeler. You like girl movies, you care about people. I wouldn't think you'd do well in a profession dedicated to killing and maiming." He still wasn't looking at her; he was too busy trying to get himself together emotionally. Neither fight nor flight was an option right now, but his heart rate wasn't buying it; it was soaring out of control.

"You should do something else," she continued. "You're too smart to be a hired gun. You're young."

"So are you. I don't see you looking to make a change."

She snorted. "I'm considerably older than you."

Her condescension stung. "Eight years isn't that much."

"And I have specific skills that translate well to this line of work."

Sam was livid. She'd just called him too young for her, too unskilled for his work, and too smart for soldiering, which insulted all of his friends. And the worst part was, she didn't seem to see it. She really thought she was being nice.

"I think you're—"

"Shut up, Macias."

She must've looked over at him finally, because her voice was louder, closer to his ear.

"What?" Her tone was incredulous.

"I said shut up. You don't know what you're talking about. I don't have to be muscle-bound or a meathead to enjoy this job or be good at it. That's stereotyping of the worst kind. Maybe militaries wouldn't make the kind of ethical mistakes they can be prone to if more people like me were a part of it, did you ever consider that? I defend people who are weak and powerless. And as for me being a feeler, yes, I am. And people like you question my toughness all the time because of it. But I'm damn good at my job. So if you have more opinions to offer on my career path, just keep them to yourself."

There was a long pause.

"Simonson. Look at me."

He wanted to turn his head. He wanted to burn his angry gaze into her soft brown one and let her absorb all that heated frustration. But he couldn't. His body was already electrified with too many sensations: the itching behind his neck from the tag on his shirt, his hurting feet, the loud music from the ballroom, the ache in his head from the mix of perfumes. He couldn't add her intense eye contact to the mix; it would combust. When he didn't turn, she went on anyway.

"There's a difference between being good at your job and being suited for it. That's all I meant."

They stood in silence until Abbie and Edward came to the doorway, saying their goodnights. Their sleepy, happy, lovesick act wasn't helping his mood, and he was relieved when they went to bed right away. He stood next to Macias the rest of the night, and for once, he didn't enjoy the silence.

TEZZA

*This could go very badly,* Tezza thought as she climbed the steps to Sam's fourth-floor apartment. Edward had stared at her when she'd asked him for Sam's address. "You're going to breach the cave of seclusion?" he'd asked, incredulous.

*Why was it so hard to understand? When you screw up and say something stupid and your friend won't return your texts, you show up at his house. You make it right. Not complicated.*

The unusual moniker for his apartment had given her pause, however. When she'd asked for landmarks, Edward shrugged.

"I've never been there," he said. "He's never invited us over."

That was the thought boiling inside her head as she knocked on his door. She could hear the TV on, so she knew he was still awake.

"Simonson. Open up. It's me." *It's me. That's what Rocco used to say when he called. I shouldn't say that to Sam.* She cleared her throat. "It's Macias."

The bolt clicked and he opened the door. He wore a red shirt that was at least one size too big, baggy cargo shorts, and white tube socks which appeared to be on inside out. *Was he in a hurry getting dressed? Did I interrupt something—does he have a girl in there?*

"What are you doing here?"

"I wanted to apologize . . ."

"You shouldn't be here, people will talk."

"I don't care about that," she said quietly. *Is that what he was yelling about the other day, during his "I hate everyone" rant?* She'd seen his friend Saint leaving shortly after.

Sam crossed his arms, not moving from the doorway. "How did you get my address?"

"I asked the king for it."

"Great." His scowl said it all. "Now I'm going to have to put up with more ballast from them, too."

"Try telling them to shut up," she said through a forced smile. "It worked on me."

"Doesn't seem like it."

*Ouch.* She took a deep breath; she wasn't leaving without getting what she came for . . . which was what, exactly? Absolution? Forgiveness? At this point, she'd settle for a return to their regularly scheduled friendship.

"May I come in?"

"Why?"

"I just want to talk to you."

Making his irritation obvious, he shuffled aside so she could enter. The low light made it hard to see, but she made her way into the living room . . . which was also the bedroom. There didn't appear to be anyone else there; it would've been impossible for them to hide. There was no couch, just a queen-size bed with a denim quilt pulled back. A video game controller and headset sat on the bed, and a large monitor was paused on some kind of fantasy role-playing game.

"Say whatever you came to say."

"I'm sorry."

"For?"

"For what I said about your suitability for your career."

"And?"

She shifted uncomfortably. She didn't usually have to talk this much. She hated it. "And that's it. Just I'm sorry." She swallowed hard, tipping her head to try to catch his gaze. *Come on, Sam, look at me.* "My assumptions were unfair. I want to get back to how things were between us. Will you forgive me?"

He opened his mouth, but the sound of sweeping orchestral music came up through the wooden floor of the apartment and he glared at the floor. Figuring she owed him something for invading his space, Tezza squatted, pressing her hands to the floor. She muttered an incantation normally used for sealing bottles of wine or jars of jam, figuring that it was more or less similar. It took a little longer, given the size of the room, but eventually, the music sounded farther and farther away, as if it were coming from a parade continuing on its route, until she couldn't hear it any longer.

"That should last a few months. I can come back and do it again if you want. Should make day sleeping easier." She touched her high ponytail, smoothing it down, wishing he'd say something, *anything*, but he just stood there, still staring at the floor, clenching his jaw.

"I'll see you Monday." She'd turned down the narrow hallway and cracked the door open, when he reached past her and slammed it shut again. When she turned, he was looking directly into her eyes.

"I will," he said, his voice soft. Tezza couldn't look away. She'd never gotten a good look at his eyes before; they were light green, so pale they were almost gray, like a pool of still water in a forest.

"You will what?" she whispered.

"Forgive you."

"Oh. Okay. Thank you."

"Sure." He shifted closer, his hand still holding the door shut, close enough that she could see the pulse point in his neck racing along at runaway train speeds. His eyes dropped to her lips. Tezza tensed. *Is he going to kiss me? He wouldn't. He can't.*

*I shouldn't let him.* But she didn't have to make the choice after all; he stepped back quickly, his eyes on the ground, opening the door for her.

"Thanks for stopping by."

"Sure. See you tomorrow."

"Yes."

### SAM

As soon as she left, Sam closed and re-locked the door, letting his forehead rest against it. *This close.* He'd come this close to kissing a married woman. That could not happen; he felt his guilt like a weight around his neck, dragging him into a sea of self-loathing. But when he'd seen her leaving like that, he'd had to stop her. Having her in his space had felt . . . right. The fact that she'd spelled his floor hadn't helped . . . She saw him. He didn't know how, but she understood his internal struggles the way no other friend ever had. *Friend. That's right, Simonson, she's a friend. And in this difficult time, she needs you to support her, just like she supports you. So remember that. And for Woz's sake, start thinking with your brain again.*

The truth was that if she hadn't been married, he'd have never allowed himself to become friends with her at all. Head still pressed against the door, he pulled out his phone.

"Saint. It's me. I need a favor."

1931 HOURS, THE NEXT NIGHT. Sam was fidgeting, rubbing the silk handkerchief in his pocket between his index finger and his thumb. "So, you're a nurse, Mei?" *Mei, like "I may like this woman." I should be able to remember that.*

His date nodded, her long black hair bobbing, as she sipped her brandy Alexander. *At least she ordered a real drink.*

"What's that like?"

"It's good. I enjoy it." Sam waited for her to elaborate. She didn't.

"How long have you been doing it?"

She blinked, and her face shifted toward amusement, but he didn't know why. "Doing what? Being a nurse?"

"Yes. How long have you been a nurse?"

She spun her tall glass slowly by its stem. "Three years, give or take."

"Huh. Where'd you study?"

"Klensingworth."

"Is that a degree program? I knew a boy in school who wanted to do that. The lads teased him mercilessly, of course."

"No, it's not a degree, just the license."

"Do you regret not going for the degree? It might've opened up different opportunities for you. For example, all the medical staff at the palace have degrees. I'm not sure about other government posts . . ."

"No, I don't regret it. I didn't have the money to go for a degree."

"Very sensible, then."

"Thank you . . ." She said it like a question.

*I've said something wrong. I wonder what it was . . .* "Have I offended you?"

Her face contorted, and a light blush appeared on her tan cheeks. "No, you just ask a lot of personal questions . . . Tell me more about the palace. What's that like?"

Sam looked around the bar, wishing he'd let Saint double with him after all. "I'm not really supposed to talk about palace life. Discretion, you know."

"But you're friends with the king, aren't you? The whole family?"

Sam took a long pull on his stout, buying time. "I am indeed friends with the king."

"That must be *amazing*," she gushed, her eyes twinkling.

Sam lifted an eyebrow. "I don't know how *amazing* it is. It's basically like my other friendships, only with fewer reciprocal financial expectations."

Mei laughed. Sam blinked. *Was that funny? I was just being candid . . . If I go home now, I wonder if I can take my drink and return the glass later. Why did I ask Saint to set me up with someone?* Just then, as if summoned by his question, Tezza walked into the bar with three other women. He almost didn't recognize her: her hair was still in that same high ponytail, but other than that . . . she wore a black leather skirt that hit her midthigh and spiked black boots with a sparkly black top that exposed her back, and he almost chuckled that once again, she couldn't seem to find another color to wear. Mei followed his stare.

"Who's that?"

"That's Macias. We met at work, we work together."

"She's very pretty," she noted.

"She's very married," he returned quickly, as he took another sip of his drink.

"Huh." Mei put her elbows on the booth's table. "Tell me more about palace life. What do you two do together?"

He watched Tezza and her friends cross to the bar and order. He replied without turning to Mei. "As I said, I'm really not at liberty to share details about palace life with you." She cleared her throat and he turned to face her, only to find Mei's face flushed again—either she'd had too much alcohol, which was unlikely, or she was angry. Sam felt his leg start to bounce.

"You needn't take offense. Look here—Macias!"

Tezza turned at his voice, searching the room for his face, and he waved her over. She strolled to their booth on her very tall boots, making it look easy. *She makes a lot of things look easy.*

"What, Simonson?"

"Would you please confirm for her that I'm not allowed to speak about palace life?"

Her eyes narrowed. "Why don't you introduce us first? That's the social convention."

*Eyes narrowed. What's she upset about? Should I not have bothered her? I hate this.*

"I apologize. Macias, this is Mei Nakahara. Mei, Tezza Macias. Mei and I were set up on a date by our mutual friend, Lieutenant Francis Saint."

Mei's face puckered to hold in a smile. "Saint's first name is Francis?"

"Yes, but he doesn't care for the name, so please don't use it."

The two women shared a look that he couldn't translate—was everyone conspiring against him tonight?—then Tezza cleared her throat.

"Nice to meet you, Mei. I can confirm that Simonson is not allowed to discuss palace life. Sorry. Tell her about your mission in Op'Ho'Lonia instead."

Sam felt his face getting hot. "Thank you for your help, Macias. Have a nice night." He doubted she was trying to embarrass him, but that was the last thing Mei needed to know about. He'd never get rid of her if she knew about his medal; she was clearly some sort of celebrity watcher.

"Wait, you're not one of the men who went after the exile, are you?"

*Damn it.* "His name is Prince Lincoln."

Mei waved a hand dismissively. "Stop with the false modesty; you're a hero! I can't believe I'm sitting here with one of the Exile Hunters! Can I get a picture with you? Do you mind?" She turned to Macias and thrust her phone toward her. Macias, however, had her arms conveniently crossed over her belly.

"No." Sam tried not to scowl. He failed miserably. "Trying to apprehend a traitor is part of my job. I don't enjoy the publicity."

"Are you joking?" Mei pulled her arm back.

"Not at all. Would you like it if I came and acted like this at the hospital? Tried to take your picture while you triage an emergency case?"

"I work in geriatrics . . ."

"Next to someone's death bed, then? Would you want to give me your autograph after you helped someone expire?"

Mei's face twisted briefly in disgust, and she sat back, digesting this. "Can't I at least see your medal?"

Sam stood up and pulled out his wallet. "Since we arrived separately, I see no reason we can't leave separately. Here's a twenty for a ride home. You can keep the change. I'll pay the bar tab as well."

Mei's mouth fell open. She looked at Macias. If Mei wanted female sympathy, she was going to have to look elsewhere: Tezza was giving the woman her patented steel gaze, clearly unmoved by the events in front of her. Looking dazed, Mei stood up, gathering her coat and her purse, and snatched the money out of his hand.

"Tell Saint this is the last time he sets me up—ever."

*Ditto,* he thought. "Certainly. Good night, Mei."

# Chapter Seven

SAM

MEI STORMED TOWARD the exit as Sam slid back into the booth and took a long drink of his stout.

"Easy, Simonson. You don't look like a man who can hold his liquor."

"I'm not going to let a perfectly good drink go to waste just because the date I was supposed to share it with ended up being unsuitable. I don't think they'll let me take the glass home, and I want to leave." Sam looked down at his shirt, disgusted; he'd worn a light-green striped button-down that he'd been told brought out his eyes. "All this effort, gone to waste."

"So stay. Get another drink and dance with my friends. They're all single."

*But you're not.* Sam's phone buzzed. "Excuse me."

**Saint: How's the date going?**

**Simonson: It's over.**

**Saint: Already?**

**Saint: Thought you picked her up at 7:00?**

**Simonson: It was long enough.**

**Saint: Mate, it's only 7:46.**

**Saint: You should've let me be your wingman.**

**Simonson: I'm not incompetent.**

**Saint: What was the problem?**

**Simonson: Why did you set me up with her?**

**Saint: She seemed reasonably smart.**

**Saint: She's in a caretaking profession, which you respect.**

**Simonson: She asked to see my medal.**

**Saint: So? That's a surefire way to get laid, mate.**

**Simonson: Conversation over.**

**Saint: Oh, come on. You could've at least snogged her.**

**Saint: Edward's poisoned your mind.**

**Simonson: For the last time, your lifestyle holds no appeal for me.**

**Simonson: Conversation over.**

Tezza cleared her throat. He was surprised to see her still standing there.

"My apologies—were you speaking to me?"

"Yes. I invited you to join my friends and me. I'm waiting for your answer." It sounded like such a simple question. Given that it was quite possibly the most difficult question he'd ever considered, Sam wished he'd been thinking about it in the back of his mind as he texted with Saint. *If I refuse, she may be hurt and offended. If I accept, I'm just torturing myself further.*

Well, given that choice . . .

"Yes, of course." Sam got up and followed her across the crowded room to a tall table where three other women sat. He recognized two of them from work; Jess handled the radios in Central Dispatch, and Victoria worked in the library. He introduced himself to the third woman, who was one of the house-keepers: Rosie.

He ordered another stout and another round for the ladies; given that they were kind enough to include him, a man so recently cast off by another woman, it seemed the least he could do.

"You have such pretty eyes," said Rosie.

"Thank you. So do you. They remind me of the casing of a computer I once had."

The ladies giggled, except Tezza, who was quiet. *No quieter than usual, though,* he told himself.

"Who gets the first dance?" Jess asked, biting her lower lip. "Do you mind, Lieutenant?"

"Not at all," he said. "I pledge to be a perfect gentleman. I'm happy to be of service."

Victoria stood and held out a hand to him, which he took. He led her to the dance floor.

"I have a confession to make," he said, taking her other hand as well. "I only know how to swing dance and slow dance."

She smiled. "That's fine, Lieutenant. Better than dancing with Rosie; she steps on my toes."

"If that's the standard, I may fail as well," he admitted. Though the music wasn't quite right, he and Victoria made it work for three songs before they both wanted a drink. Tezza had ordered them water, and Sam hadn't yet finished his when Rosie was dragging him back to the center of the pub. She put his hand on her hip and grabbed the other and did most of the leading; it seemed just as well. He was sweating and ready for a rest when he came back for his water, but Jess had been waiting so long, he felt guilty for putting her off. She was easiest to talk to by far, since she turned out to be a gamer. He'd always thought she seemed quite comfortable in a headset; that must be why. He plopped down on his stool and gulped his water and started on his stout when he felt three sets of eyes staring at him. Rosie cleared her throat meaningfully. Jess tipped her head toward Tezza, who was staring into her drink. *Oh. Right.*

He stood up. "Macias, your turn."

She flipped her hair back and looked up. *Eyebrows close together, mouth grimacing, head tipped.* He had no idea what she was thinking. The other three piped up immediately, gently pushing her off her stool, promising to watch her purse and let no one steal her drink. He held out a hand, and she laced her fingers with his.

"Apologies in advance," he said, as he headed back toward the middle of the room. "As the final partaker of my dancing skills, you bear the brunt of my sweatiness."

Macias shrugged one shoulder. "That's fine."

It was a slow song. He kept her right hand in his left, pressing it to his chest, curling his fingers around hers, and guided her closer to him. He could smell that same plumeria shampoo and something else—perfume, maybe? It was definitely floral. Her companions were grinning at him, and he cocked an eyebrow. Since he was used to standing in silence with Macias, he didn't attempt to fill it with conversation. Sam's muscles felt loose, his feet heavy; the soft skin of her back reminded him of a stone pounded by the waves until you could see the oils your fingers left in trails. It hit him how he'd never fully appreciated the shape of her body until this moment, with it pressed against his; he wanted to run his hands over her curves, explore the highs and lows of her terrain like he was making a map. During the second song, she let her chin rest near his neck, her hair tickling his cheek. He was still taller than her in her tall boots, but not by much. He thought about making a joke about bringing stilts next time. But then he realized, there likely would not be a next time. With that unfortunate thought, he decided to say nothing at all.

"Thanks," she muttered as the song ended.

"We can do a third, if you like." He searched her dark eyes. He'd never been less sure what someone's expression meant; he could've sworn that he saw longing, maybe grief. *Why would dancing with me cause her pain? Does it remind her of Rocco?* Yet the way she leaned into him, the way she'd played with his collar . . . he was positive she'd enjoyed the closeness, too, positive she wanted to stay.

"No. Thank you."

"Okay." He squeezed her hand, but she looked away. She turned and hurried back to the table, and he trailed after her more slowly.

"Well," Sam said, "it seems I've served my purpose. Can I trust you ladies to see each other safely home? No man left behind, right?"

"My father's going to pick us up after," said Victoria.

"Excellent." He paused, his eyes on Tezza. Something had shifted between them; there had been a trust in the way she'd leaned into him, the way she'd threaded their fingers together. "Macias?" Her whiskey gaze lifted to his, and it was just as intoxicating as his stout had been. "Are you . . . I mean, are we . . ." He sighed. "Never mind." As soon as the words were out of his mouth, he realized his mistake. Sam quickly grabbed his coat and turned to leave. He thought he was off the hook until he heard her call after him.

"One hundred push-ups, Simonson." He turned to find her wearing a small smirk, still staring into her drink.

"What, here?"

"Yes. Here." She lifted her gaze to his. "Or you can finish that sentence. Your choice." *Impossible,* he thought, since he was so befuddled he didn't even know what he'd been trying to ask. Setting his jacket back down with a sigh, he rolled up his sleeves, muttering under his breath.

"Are you going to count?"

"Of course."

"I don't know what this is," Jess announced, "but I love it." She got up and came around the table to see him better. All four women and half the pub started counting for him. His arms started to burn around seventy-five, and the floor was unpleasantly sticky, but he certainly wasn't going to lose face in front of her friends. When they finally shouted "One hundred!" the whole pub broke into applause. With a small smile, Tezza gave him a friendly head jerk as he headed back out onto the cool street. *We're okay. Good.* His phone buzzed.

**Saint: You head home?**

**Simonson: No. I stayed and danced with four women.**

**Saint: SHOW THEM YOUR MEDAL.**

**Simonson: Good night, Francis.**

TEZZA

A KNOCK AT THE DOOR startled Tezza out of a nice dream. *Noon? Who could be here at noon? Everyone knows I'm asleep.* She checked her phone; no missed calls. The unknown person knocked again, more insistently, and she stumbled out of her bedroom to the front door. Her mind was still lingering in the dream where she'd been dancing with Sam, feeling his heat against her, his big hands on her back, his lips on her neck . . . She whipped the door open and tried to focus.

"Mrs. Macias?" There was a soldier at her front door. An Op'Ho'Lonian soldier. A colonel.

"Yes?"

"May I come in?"

"Yes." She stood aside, running a hand through her unruly hair as he entered her small bungalow. *This is it. He's going to tell me what he's found out. He's going to lay to rest all my questions; I'm going to breathe for the first time in . . .* Tezza had to do some math in her head. When had she stopped counting the days? *Two years, 195 days.* "Can I get you something to drink?"

"No, thank you, ma'am." He took off his beret and held it in front of him. "Would you please sit down?"

"He's dead, isn't he?"

His stoic expression cracked a little. "Ma'am. Please sit."

She sat on her blue velvet couch, the one she bought when she moved here eighteen months ago to be closer to her sister, Alba. They'd found it at a thrift shop downtown and convinced the conductor to let them take it on the train so they didn't have to hire a wagon. Other passengers took turns taking selfies with it; two girls made out on it at one point. Her life already had a history that didn't include Rocco . . . and now, perhaps a future without him as well.

"Is there someone you can call to be with you?"

Sam's face popped into her mind. *No, I should call Alba. I don't want the colonel to get the wrong impression.* With shaking hands, she texted Alba, who promised to dump the girls on a neighbor and be right over.

"She'll be here soon."

"Thank you, ma'am."

"Are you sure I can't get you anything?"

"Yes, ma'am, I'm sure."

Though it was against her usual nature to make small talk with strangers, the dark fear that was swelling inside her demanded a sacrifice, and the silence was the only one available.

"Did you serve with my husband, colonel?"

"Yes, ma'am. Two tours."

"Across the Sparkling Sea?"

"Yes, ma'am, and the Cortesian uprising in New Pyet as well. He was a good man." The colonel paled, probably realizing he'd used the past tense by mistake. Tezza heard it, too, and the tears came.

"Yes, he was," she said softly.

"He was faithful to you, ma'am." Tezza looked up from staring at her folded hands, her vision still blurred.

"How so?" It didn't matter now, of course; but after all these years, effectively single but unable to move on, it would help a little to hear that he'd suffered a similar fate, even briefly.

"One night in New Pyet, they brought in these girls . . ." He shook his head at the memory, his eyes wide. Tezza smiled a little. "Never seen girls like these before in all my days. They were perfect, one in every style . . . Rocco never even looked at them. One of the girls tried to get into his tent, and he slapped her backside and sent her howling to the commander."

She was laughing and crying at the same time. Crying with relief; it was over, the waiting was over. Laughing over the happy memory of a good man who'd loved her.

"Did he suffer?"

He blanched. "Your sister should be here . . ."

"I'm fine, Colonel. Just tell me, please."

"We don't believe so," he said. "He was taken prisoner, but according to another prisoner who was recently released, he contracted brain bender fever, and he was gone within days of being captured."

"So he died years ago."

"Yes, ma'am."

She covered her face with both hands. It was too much. She had hoped that if he was still alive he wasn't suffering somewhere, but just knowing that he'd been gone all this time . . . She wiped both cheeks of tears.

"Colonel, I'm going to have some sangria. Sure you don't want any?"

"You go right ahead, ma'am."

She was already pretty buzzed by the time Alba got there, and not wanting to listen again, Tezza went to lie down while he rehashed all the details for her sister. His voice bled down the hall nonetheless; he left out the story about the prostitutes. After he left, Alba came into her dark bedroom and lay down next to her.

"Nic can handle the kids. I'm going to stay here tonight. I'll braid your hair if you want."

Tezza snorted, the allusion to a childish slumber party ritual feeling completely at odds with the adult situation she now found herself in, and it started the tears again.

"Pretty rude of you to drink all the sangria. Good thing I brought the ingredients for more."

"I'll be sick if I drink more."

"More for me, then." Alba sighed, combing her fingers through Tezza's hair. "Woz, he was a good man. He didn't deserve to die that way. You didn't deserve to wait three years just to find out he was long gone."

"I don't think deserving has much to do with it. It happened."

"Makes you think, though, yes? Life is precious."

Tezza nodded, wiping her runny nose on her sleeve. "Yes. It's precious." She released a heavy sigh. "Being here with you, doing work I enjoy, it helped. Thank you for pestering me into coming to this strange place."

"They're all going to offer you tea, you know. Orangies think tea fixes everything."

"Oh Woz! Oh no," Tezza groaned. "I was supposed to meet Simonson for coffee before work. Get my phone. I have to call him or he'll come over."

"Simonson, the guy I met?"

"Yes. The caffeine keeps us awake."

"I didn't know you were dating."

"How could we be dating, I'm ma—" The word died on her tongue, and she swallowed hard. "We're just friends . . . Where's my jacking phone?"

"He's got a girlfriend, then?"

"No, he hates when strangers check him out. Avoids peopling around with people. I can't talk about Sam right now, I have to get changed."

"Tez, you can't go to work like this."

"No, I want to. I can't just mope around."

"Tezzarina, you're kinda drunk. I don't think they'll want you guarding the grand duchess like this." She made a fair point, but she still had to let Sam know what had happened. Alba convinced her to text instead of calling.

**Macias: Can't come to coffee, sorry. Got news about Rocco.**

**Simonson: He's alive?**

**Macias: No, dead. A long time dead. So dead.**

**Simonson: Are you okay? Who's with you?**

**Macias: Alba's here. I'm a little drinky, but I'm okay.**

**Simonson: A little "drinky" is understandable in these circumstances. I'm so sorry. Please tell your sister I can come over in the morning if she has to work.**

**Macias: No, she don't work. Doesn't work. LOL**

**Simonson: All right, I'll let work know that you won't be in.**

**Simonson: Okay to tell the grand duchess?**

**Macias: Sure. Why not.**

**Simonson: I'll call you tomorrow, all right?**

**Macias: Okay.**

# Chapter Eight

SAM

*MISTAKE. MISTAKE. MISTAKE,* his brain chanted as he walked to Tezza's house. She'd been gone from work for three days, and it was time to check on her in person. He'd texted her that he was coming, but going to her house right now was still a social minefield; he was bound to make some mistakes. His chest ached with the prospect of seeing her again. People were bound to see. *But this is what friends do,* he argued back. *Friends comfort each other when they're hurting. I can do this. I'm the right man for the job. She doesn't know the others very well; Abbie is her employer, for heaven's sake. I'm the one it made sense to send.* He knocked, but no one answered. He rang the bell. Hurrying footsteps came to the door, and she peeked out the small window in the door. He wanted to wave, but his hands were full. *Why did I bring so much stuff? This is their fault.*

She opened the door, still squeezing her wet black hair into a towel. She wore a loose brown cable-knit sweater that hung off one shoulder and white shorts. Her hair was naturally wavy, apparently; she must have been straightening it most mornings. The loose curls were a good look for her, and he felt the tightness in his chest ease at the sight of her face.

"You showered. That's good."

She quirked an eyebrow as he came inside without being invited. "Why?"

"People who are grieving often don't take care of themselves."

Tezza sobered. "Grieving?"

"Yes. For your husband. I've brought gifts of comfort."

Her eyes went to the potted plant and he thrust it forward.

"This is from the grand duchess. She insisted that I bring flowers. I decided that was overly sentimental, not to mention impractical as cut flowers only last an average of a week unless properly maintained; even then, it's two weeks at best. This spider plant requires very little watering or care and should last for years to come." She took it with a small smile on her face. "I didn't think about your affinity for plants when I purchased it; if you'd like something more ornate, that can be arranged."

"No," she said quickly, "this is good. Thanks, Simonson."

He scowled. "I told you, it's from the grand duchess. Thank *her*."

She smiled wider. "Okay, I will." *Such a gorgeous smile . . . Focus, Simonson.*

"There's more." He let his backpack slide off his shoulder. "The guys wanted to send you junk food so you could 'eat your feelings.' Their words." He pulled out an insulated lunch box. "They suggested chocolate everything, but I thought you might appreciate some variety. One can only eat so much chocolate, after all." He pulled out the coffee gelato. "In your country of origin, this is popular."

"Yes, it is," she said quietly. "I—"

"The quality here probably isn't as good. Sorry about that. But I got you potato chips. They're not traditional, but they're tasty. And I did get chocolate chip cookies and chocolate chips and uncooked chocolate chip cookie dough, so you can tailor that experience to your liking. The budget wasn't an issue because of Edward's share, but they were on sale. That's hard to pass up. Grieving people often don't eat enough, so the high calorie values shouldn't be an issue if you're concerned about your body's shape and size."

Sam heard a sniffle as he took a breath. He looked up sharply. Tezza was crying. He pulled her toward him by her elbows, searching her face.

"What's wrong? Is it too much? I knew it was too much."

"No," she laughed through her tears, wiping her eyes. "I'm just . . . I'm touched."

"Oh." He scrutinized her face: eyebrows high, mouth smiling but lip also trembling a little, a few tears, but not a river, expression open and sincere. *This is what touched looks like.* "Oh, well, that's okay, then. But just wait, because my present is better than all those combined."

She lifted an eyebrow, and he grinned. "You're going to regret your skepticism, Macias."

"As I recall, you plan to annihilate it."

"Still working on it." He went back into his backpack and pulled out the wrapped book. She went over to a blue velvet couch and sat down as she opened the gift, and he sat next to her. He took a good look around the room for the first time. The floors were wood, distressed from use, not simply to be fashionable, and the rug was handwoven in warm oranges, rusty reds, and the same dark blue. Her coffee table had a nice arrangement of candles in ceramic tiled containers. Her bookcase was twisted like a tree, reaching up to the ceiling. Her style fit her perfectly; intense but warm. He was so busy looking around, he missed her initial reaction.

"Oh, wow. *501 Ways to Injure a Man without Touching Him.* I've heard this is great."

"I thought it would be appropriate for you. Something to read on your flight. My only caveat is that you can't use any of it on me or my friends."

"You'd make an excellent test subject."

"Nevertheless."

She was smiling at him, and he smiled back. *I don't know what they were so worried about.*

"You seem like you're doing well, considering your circumstances. I'm glad."

She ran a hand through her hair. "Grief is a sine wave. I'm okay now; I wasn't great last night. I realized how many things I was saving for when he came back. And now he never is." She swiped her fingers under her eyes. "But in other ways, I grieved his loss a long time ago. Thank you for the gifts of comfort. They are very appreciated." She was looking at him funny. He'd seen James make that face at Dr. Broward when her back was turned.

"What's your expression mean?"

She seemed startled; he did know that one. "What?"

"You said I could ask you about facial expressions. I don't know that one."

"I . . . it's . . . I did say that, didn't I?"

"Yes. On our third night of work together when we discussed each other's strengths and weaknesses."

"Can I ask you to forget it?"

His eyes narrowed. "Only if you want to give me one hundred push-ups."

She chuckled. "I don't have the energy for that right now; I could do fifty, maybe."

"I understand; grief is tiring. You can postpone payment until your first day back at work." He stood up, looking around for his stuff. "The article I read on visiting grieving people said not to stay too long. I should go."

"Hey, Simonson?" He turned back to her. "Can I ask a favor?"

"Of course. Anything."

"I have to go to Op'Ho'Lonia for the funeral. Normally, I'd ask my sister to stop by the house, but she'll be with me, and it's ten days. I don't want to mess up your routines, don't know what else is going on in your life, but . . ."

"I'd be happy to watch your house."

She nodded. "You don't have to stay here. Just come by and get the mail and feed the fish and water my plants."

"Please leave detailed instructions, and I will follow them to the letter. I make no guarantees, for I'm not great with animals, but fish seem fairly simple creatures and not apt to cause too much—"

She leaned forward and kissed him. Not on the cheek, as he'd seen Edward do with his sisters. Not on the forehead, as he'd seen Abbie do to Simon. It would've felt innocent to a more experienced man, a gentle press of her lips to his without drama or seduction in mind, just a sweet gesture of gratitude. But to a twenty-two-year-old who'd never dated as an adult, it felt like a lit fuse. He stared at her, wide-eyed, all appropriate words evaporating from his mind.

"Holy shit, Macias." She gave him a small smile. "What . . . what are you . . ."

"Thanks for watching the house. Here's a key. I'll print off the instructions and email you a copy; I know you like that." *She's just going right on talking. Am I having some sort of psychological break with reality? Is this what hallucinating feels like?* She was watching him expectantly.

"Yeah, I . . . I do, I like having a digital copy," he stammered, his voice sounding vacant to his own ears.

"I leave tomorrow and I'll be back late afternoon Saturday after next. Back to work Sunday night."

"Macias."

"Yes, Simonson?" Her expression was still open, searching.

"You kissed me, right? That happened?"

"Yes." She picked up his backpack and handed it to him. He slung it over one shoulder as she herded him toward the door. "Thank you again for the gifts, and I'll be sure to thank the other contributors as well."

"Yes. Okay. Good. See you on . . ."

"Sunday. The second."

"Yes, Sunday." He stumbled out the front door. "Sunday. Have a good trip."

"Thanks, Sam." She smiled as she closed the door behind him.

AFTER TEZZA KISSED him, Sam didn't go home. He caught a train to Bluffton immediately. Dean and Georgie were outside the door to the residence, so he knew the royals were home. They saw the look on his face and let him in immediately. Edward and Abbie were watching a horror movie—Abbie must have found out she'd won the bet, after all—his arm slung around her, her head on his shoulder, their feet up on the coffee table. On the screen, a young woman was creeping toward a door at the end of a hallway, which had red smoke coming out around the edges.

"Hey."

They both jumped, and in spite of his weird afternoon, he laughed.

"Woz, Sam, are you trying to kill us? Don't sneak up on us like that," Edward berated, turning on a light to see him better as Abbie paused the film. "Are you here for work already?"

He shook his head, taking a hesitant step into the room. "I need advice." He swallowed. "She kissed me."

At this, Abbie sat up straight. "Was it the flowers? I knew flowers would do it."

He scowled. "I didn't get flowers, I got her a spider plant. And she loved it, by the way."

Abbie groaned, massaging her temples. "Sam, I said flowers for a reason. Flowers are sentimental, romantic . . . Spider plants are practical and boring."

"Well, she loved it. And the book, and the junk food, all of it. And then she got a weird look on her face, and I asked her what it meant, and she was evasive and promised me one hundred push-ups later . . ."

"Wait a minute," Edward said, holding his hands up. "You lost me, mate. Push-ups?"

"Yeah, it's this thing we do where if someone starts to say something and then says 'never mind,' you have to do one hundred push-ups. Macias and her husband used to . . ." He sat down hard on the ottoman. "What am I doing? She's married."

"Not anymore," Abbie said softly.

"Perhaps that's the message she was trying to send with her kiss. Do you think she was signaling availability?" Edward asked.

Sam sighed. "Maybe."

"What preceded the kiss? Let's analyze it," his friend prompted.

Abbie gave them an exaggerated eye roll. Edward ignored her, so Sam did, too.

"I said I would watch her house while she's gone for the funeral, and we were discussing the necessary duties when she suddenly kissed me . . ."

"Kissed your cheek?"

"No, my lips."

Edward's mouth fell open in surprise. "Just like that?"

"Yes!" Sam threw his hands up in the air. "Just like that!"

"That brazen hussy," Abbie deadpanned, shaking her head.

"Do I need to send you somewhere else, woman? We're having a serious conversation here," Edward grumped, and Abbie grinned.

"Just try it, Your Majesty."

Edward glared at her, then turned back to Sam. "And then what happened?"

"She just went on talking like nothing had happened. I even confirmed with her that she'd just done what I thought she just did, and she just—"

"Hang on, you two," Abbie said, pulling out her phone, dialing. "We don't have the right person in this conversation."

"Who are you—" Edward started to ask, and she held up a finger to ask for silence.

"Hello?" Saint's deep voice came through the speaker-phone. *She's right*, thought Sam. *We need a player in this discussion.*

"Hey, it's Abbie. Quick question for you."

"Go."

"What does it mean when a woman kisses you in the middle of a conversation and then goes right back to what she was talking about?"

"Am I seeing her?"

"No, she's just a friend."

"Oh. Then she doesn't want to be just friends anymore, but she doesn't want to screw up the friendship, so she's testing the waters. Was there tongue?"

Sam shook his head, and Abbie verbalized, "No."

"It could be she's just very openly affectionate, but more likely, she wants more. Friends with benefits, maybe."

Sam felt his eyes go wide. "*Benefits?* Oh Jersey, no, I can barely handle regular friendship, I do *not* think we need to add *benefits* into the mix . . ."

"Who's that, Sam? Who's kissing Sam? That hot security chick?"

"Bye, Saint, gotta go."

"Wait, who's kissing—"

Abbie hung up.

Edward shook his head. "Why do you torture the poor man?"

"I'm mad at him. He was supposed to take me to the weapons range last week and he bailed at the last minute for a date with Lieutenant Paris."

Edward gave her a hard look. "I don't know if I want you going to the weapons range."

"Yeah, I know. That's why I asked *him*."

Sam clapped his hands. "Focus, you two. I need help."

"Sorry," Abbie said. "Did you kiss her back?"

He shook his head. "I was too shocked."

"Did you kiss her before you left? Give her any kind of positive reaction?"

"I said 'holy shit,' I think. She kind of pushed me out the door."

"Yeah," Abbie snickered, "that sounds like T. She's a mystery." She pulled out her phone again, deleting texts from Saint with requests for more information. "This strange face she made. Let's unpack that."

"I don't know. She looked kind of scared, but happy."

"Nostrils flared?"

"Yeah, a little."

"Cheeks pink?"

"Yes."

"Pupils dilated?"

"I don't like looking into people's eyes . . ."

Abbie leaned forward. "I know, Sam. But those are all attraction nonverbals. Tezza probably likes you. She wouldn't explain her face because she wasn't sure how you felt. But she put the ball in your court. And you've got ten days to figure out what you want to do with it."

Sam stood up and scrubbed a hand over his face. "I'm going home now."

"Don't you have to work in an hour?"

"Oh. Yeah."

"Stay," Abbie said. "I'll cook you some dinner. Or breakfast, or whatever. We never see you anymore, apart from our morning greetings. I'll put something else on the TV if the horror film bothers you . . ."

Edward's eyes were pleading, and he mouthed the words, "Please stay. Please, please, please," and Sam sat down between them on the couch, shaking his head.

"Fine. I will stay, but I'm sitting between you so there's no funny business. I'll take two eggs sunny side up, firm yolks, with crisp bacon and strong coffee." Abbie practically skipped across the room to her kitchen.

WHEN SAM STEPPED OUTSIDE to start his shift, he groaned. Saint was standing there, arms folded across his wide chest, wearing a Cheshire grin.

"Hello, ladies' man," he said in his deepest register. "How was *your* day?"

"Get out of here. I'm working."

"Me too. I'm filling in for Macias," he said, "so we've got plenty of time to talk."

"Macias and I don't talk when we work."

"No, there's better ways to pass the time, apparently . . ."

"Hey!" Sam felt his face flush. "We weren't working, we were at her house! We would never do that on duty; she's a total professional. She's on bereavement leave because she just found out her husband is *dead*, remember?"

"Wait a minute. She finds out her husband is dead, and the first thing she does is kiss you?"

Sam said nothing. This whole situation was getting out of hand.

"Damn, Sammy. You better jump on that."

Sam shook his head. Now that he'd eaten something, he'd cleared his head, gained some perspective. "She was just grateful. That's all." He lowered his voice. "Why would she want to be with me? I'm a hot mess when it comes to women."

"Which is why you should *jump on it* if a woman's into your brand of crazy."

"Conversation over."

"Sam, come on. I just meant—"

"Conversation over."

"I know it's delicate, working together, but you could easily—"

"Conversation over."

"You've got twelve hours to pick my brain, which is *chock full of information about women*, and you just want to stand here in silence?"

"That's correct."

"Fine." That's what they did . . . for a while.

Around 2300 hours, when Edward and Abbie had gone to bed, apparently without breaking any more lamps, Sam cleared his throat.

"My life is carefully ordered."

"Yeah?"

"Yes. In ways not even you guys know about. I don't know if there's room for a woman in my life. I can't imagine what woman would want that, want me."

"Give me an example."

"I can't sleep without a heavy blanket on me."

He heard Saint's clothes shift as he shrugged. "A lot of people like the covers on them . . ."

"Mine weighs twenty pounds."

"Huh."

"When I'm at home, I wear my clothes inside out so the seams don't drive me crazy."

Saint was silent for a moment. "Does that mean that your clothes drive you crazy when you're out?"

"You're missing the point. The point is I'm not normal."

"What's normal? My parents are Imaharan, and they adopted a white kid. That's not normal."

"But your parents are great."

"Of course they are. But the point is that everyone's weird somehow. What's really weird are the people who think their brand of crazy is normal." He paused. "Does she know?"

"She knows some of it."

"And?"

"And she doesn't seem to care."

"You don't have to marry her next week, Sam. Try the relationship on for size, see how she fits. It's called dating."

"Yes, and like carbon dating, it has a rate of decay. When it doesn't work out, and we have to stand here in silence every night for twelve hours, that's gonna be terrible."

"I thought you were doing that master's certificate, the risk assessment thing?"

He'd applied for it after Tezza told him he was too smart to be in the military. And he'd been accepted, but he'd deferred it, saying the timing wasn't right. And standing there next to Saint, he realized the only reason the timing hadn't been right was that he was too busy spending all night standing next to a woman who really interested him, who he really liked standing next to. A woman he wouldn't see anymore if he were back in school.

"I might."

"So, then you wouldn't work together."

"I'd still see her every time we're with Abbie at night."

"Maybe not. Maybe she'll quit now that her husband's been found."

He hadn't thought of that. *How did that not occur to me? Of course she'll go back to Op'Ho'Lonia. She was just killing time here with us. She's going to get on with her life, far, far away from here, with someone else.*

"Take it easy, man. I can hear you hyperventilating from over here."

He looked at Saint. "But what if she quits? I don't want her to quit. Abbie needs her."

"Tell her that."

He flexed his jaw. "I will."

"Just didn't realize you'd changed your name to Abbie."

Sam scowled at him. He'd shove him, but he'd just end up in a head lock again.

# Chapter Nine

TEZZA

"MAMA."

"Tezzarina," her mother cried, tears already on her cheeks. She embraced her, and Tezza smelled the cheap grocery store perfume that she always wore, and she breathed deep in the scent of her childhood and pulled as much comfort from it as she could. "I am sorry, so sorry, my dear girl. Rocco was a gem, he was gold. We will miss him so."

Tezza just nodded. Alba was at her elbow, handing her her suitcase. "Oh. Thanks." She was usually asleep now, of course; it was 1100 hours, and she felt fuzzy. Tezza mentally touched the magic curling at her ankles, and though it didn't know her well anymore, it responded beautifully, pouring energy into her, co-cooning around her like a fuzzy, familiar blanket. That small mercy, it brought tears to her eyes. It would be good to be with her family this week. To remember Rocco with people who'd known him.

As she'd known they would, her family swept her into their comfortable, bossy embrace. Her father took her suitcase without asking her. Her mother pushed her hair out of her face. Alba fussed at everyone the whole ride home, and her brothers and their wives and kids were all waiting at her parents' big house. Her sister-in-law pressed a bowl of food into her hands, and she smelled the sweet paprika, spicy sausage, saffron. The thick scent of herbs made her think of Sam's reaction to his omelet, and she smiled a little.

"It's good, yes?" Carlita noticed her smile.

Tezza nodded, digging into it, hoping Carlita wouldn't also notice that she'd yet to take her first bite. Her niece clamped onto her leg, and Tezza patted her head before dragging the two of them to the back door to sit outside; the weather was unseasonably warm, and the child ran off to play in the yard with her cousins.

Her brother Marcos greeted her with a cheek kiss. "You look great, sis." He didn't talk like they had growing up; he'd affected an Attaamish accent and vocabulary that their mother lamented behind his back.

"Thanks."

"You're supposed to look like Jersey. Try harder."

She grinned at him, shaking her head. "Sorry." She swallowed her bite. "I am sad. I am. But I'm also . . ."

"Relieved?"

"Yes. Relieved. The waiting killed me. I'd feel dead inside, and then some small thing would resurrect me, bring my hopes alive again. Only to die again when it went nowhere. My love has lived and died again a thousand times in three years."

"Shit," he muttered, and she didn't know why, but it made her feel better. He pulled her into a hug.

SHE'D BEEN ASSIGNED to sleep in the study on the pull-out couch. There were picture books and stuffed animals on it, and she knocked them off, too exhausted to care. Tezza picked up a laundry basket to move it. One part of it came away in her hands, and the clothes spilled out the side as her mother walked in with sheets and towels for her.

"Mama. What's happening with this basket?"

Flor tsked. "You didn't get both parts."

"Why does a laundry basket have two parts?"

Her mother adopted a patronizing tone. "They are the same kind of basket, you see? This one is broken, on the side." She pointed to the basket still on the ground. "This one is also broken at the bottom. But if I put them together, since they are broken differently, the clothes stay in."

She didn't know if the metaphor was really that profound, or if she was just insanely tired and jet-lagged, but Tezza started to laugh. *If I put them together, since they are broken differently* . . . That was just it. Between her depression and his social struggles, they were both different, both a mess sometimes. *But together* . . . Together, they could be okay. He'd hold her when she was sad. She'd remind him not to ask probing questions if he'd just met someone. He'd help her reclaim her relationship with magic. She'd buy him shirts with flat seams that wouldn't bother his skin. It could work. She just knew. She felt it deep down, this calm, wordless assurance that together, their struggles wouldn't matter so much.

Her mother was watching her with alarm, and Tezza covered her face with her hands, shoulders shaking, and let her laughter turn to tears.

"Yes, Tezzarina, yes, cry," Flor said, gathering her into a tight hold. "Cry for your husband. This is good, this is good." Her mother rubbed her back, and Tezza felt shame flood her heart. She should be crying for Rocco and not because she was falling for her coworker. She wanted to tell her mom the truth

. . . but right then, it felt good to just be held. She'd correct the misunderstanding later. Possibly from a different country, where she wouldn't have to dodge blows to her face.

The next morning, she did cry for Rocco. She cried when she saw the beautiful flowers people had sent to the church for the service. She cried when she saw his parents. They looked so much older; she hadn't seen them or his siblings in over a year. She cried when the military presented her with a flag. She cried when they did a ten-gun salute due to his Special Forces status; she was touched by that. She cried when they served lunch, because it was all Rocco's favorites: spicy sausage, thin-cut french fries, coleslaw. It was totally unseasonal, and no one seemed to care. She cried as she went through his clothes and possessions. *I don't want to give all this away. I want to keep some of it, somehow.*

"Papa." Her father looked up from the book he was reading to the gang of grandchildren he'd attracted. "When you're done, I need to ask you something."

She went back to the boxes of old music recordings and books and sharp shooter awards from his school days. Their fading love letters, which he'd printed out from emails "for posterity." His were always more romantic. Words had never come easily to her.

Her father's hand on her shoulder startled her. She wiped her face again.

"Papa, I want to bury these things in the woods." She swallowed as his eyes went shiny, too. Her dad had always been a softie. *More like Sam,* she realized. "I didn't get to bury Rocco, but I still need . . . closure."

"Of course, of course. I'll have the boys dig a hole."

"No," she said. "Just point me to a shovel. I'll do it myself."

He frowned. "There will be roots, rocks. Let them help. Let them . . ." Something in her expression stopped him, apparently. Without another word, he turned to the wall and pulled off a spade and a pickax. "When you are finished, please call us. We will come stand with you."

She nodded. She didn't bother changing; she was already going to throw this dress away. It was filthy from going through the boxes in the attic, anyway.

At one foot deep, her shoulders began to burn. At two feet deep, blisters bloomed on the pads of her palms. The roots were as thick as her wrist in places; she brought the spade high and plunged it into the hole with all her strength over and over, raging at it. *How could you leave me alone? How dare you go on without me? You were supposed to come home. You promised me, promised me, promised me,* her heart chanted as she struggled to see the hole through tears, her muscles shouting with the strain. Tezza sang the funeral dirge with the motion of her body. She hadn't had a depth in mind for the hole, but at three feet, she felt calm again. Spent. The tears had stopped. It was big enough. She could feel her family members hovering at the edge of the lawn where the wild wood took over, drinking, chatting to cover the fact that they were keeping watch over her. When she motioned them over, they left the children inside with the television.

She set the box of favorite things in the hole. She wiped her sweaty brow with her shoulder.

"Would anyone like to say anything?" her father asked.

Javier raised his hand, stepped forward shyly. "Thanks for teaching me about girls," he muttered, and everyone smiled.

His wife, Bianca, piped up. "Yes, thanks, Rocco. Before you? Hopeless."

Javier laughed with them, blushing, then stopped. "Seriously, though. You gave great advice. You were more than a brother-in-law. You were a brother. Thanks."

Tezza's tears came back. How was she not a withered husk right now from dehydration? As if she were wondering the same thing, her mother pressed a glass of ice water into her hand. She took it gratefully.

"He cooked a mean frittata," said Alba. "Remember that? When I had Valentia? Tezza was off training, so he brought me frittatas, made sure we were fed. I think he even did laundry."

"Glad he tried it at least once," Tezza muttered, and everyone chuckled. "No, he helped out when he was home. I shouldn't say that. I've missed that." She turned to the box. "I've missed you. I've missed you so much, Roc. I love you. I hope you've found peace."

They stood in silence, listening to the wind in the tops of the trees, shushing them. Her father started to sing an old spiritual; she hadn't thought of it in years.

*Who knows where the wind comes from, or where the wind goes?*

*When I leave here, I'll follow wherever it blows.*

*For where it blows leads to the one my heart knows.*

*Where it blows, surely, the one my heart chose.*

She closed her eyes. They sang it again, and she heard someone pick up the shovel and start moving the dirt back in.

HER PARENTS' HOUSE had been quiet after the funeral. Her siblings mostly went back to their normal jobs and routines, except Nic and Alba and their kids, who were staying in the house. So it was a bit of a surprise when on her last full day in Op'Ho'Lonia, Tezza came downstairs to find all five of her siblings sitting around the kitchen table. All the conversation stopped abruptly when she came into the room.

"Good morning."

"Good morning," they all mumbled, drinking their coffee, picking at croissants. She poured herself a cup and leaned against the counter to glare at them.

"Are you having an intervention?"

They gave half-hearted laughs and shrugs.

"Who's it for?" She suddenly heard the quiet in the house; no wonder she'd slept in. She looked around. "Where are all the kids?"

"Out to breakfast with Yaya and Yayo."

Javier nudged Marcos, her oldest brother, and he cleared his throat.

"First of all, we love you, sis . . ."

Tezza choked on her coffee. "I'm sorry; the intervention is for *me*?" She dabbed pointlessly at the brown speckles on her white T-shirt.

"It's not an intervention, more like . . . encouragement. Solidarity."

"Yes, solidarity," Alba echoed, and they all bobbed their heads like pigeons. "Come sit down."

Making her face stony, Tezza sat stiffly between Miquel and Alba on the bench.

"We love you, sis," Marcos started again. "We loved him, too. But there's nothing to wait for anymore. It's time to move on with your life. You're our baby sister, but you're not so young anymore. It's not about a romance, necessarily, but . . . just, find a life that pleases you. Makes you happy. And if you find somebody else, somebody new, that's great, too."

She sat back, her arms crossed.

"We would've taken longer to let you grieve, but we're so rarely all together . . . It seemed like an opportunity to talk to you as a family."

*And you were all too chicken to do it alone.*

Tezza nodded, slowly. She understood what they were trying to say. It still felt too soon—in some ways, her grief was just starting—but she appreciated how much they cared, even if they didn't understand. They knew they were risking her wrath.

She leaned forward and took the croissant off Marcos's plate as punishment for making her feel things, shoving the whole thing into her mouth so she wouldn't have to talk. Alba looked like she was about to explode, her lips pinched together.

"What?" Tezza asked around her stolen croissant.

"Can we talk about Sam? Please say yes, I've wanted to say something since we got here."

Her brothers perked up in unison.

"Who's Sam?"

"Is she seeing someone?"

"How long has this been going on?"

Tezza felt her pulse pounding; it was one thing to share this information with Alba, her big sister who would keep her secrets, and quite another to share it with all her brothers. She looked around for a quick reason to leave.

Antonio crossed his arms in playful perturbation. "How come Alba's met this Sam and we haven't?"

Tezza lifted her chin. "If you ever *visited* . . ."

Her brothers launched into loud protests about their work responsibilities, and she shushed them.

"Sam is my coworker." *There. That should be enough information for them.*

"So, what's he like?" The brothers had turned to Alba, who appeared more than willing to dish.

"He's kind of shy, but very sweet. A little unusual. Rather handsome, very good-hearted. He takes her to coffee, he fixes things in her house."

"A competent man," Miquel said, and the others nodded. "What else?"

"She calls him 'petunia,' which annoys him." Alba cast a sidelong glance at her, smirking.

"You know," Marcos said, spinning his empty coffee cup, "in our history, petunias were thought to keep away evil spirits. When given as a gift, they can symbolize being comfortable with a person . . . Did you know that, Tezzarina?"

Tezza ignored him, taking Antonio's croissant this time.

Alba went on. "And he brought her presents when he heard about Rocco."

"What kind of presents?" Javier asked, leaning closer. They waited for Tezza to answer this time.

"Coffee gelato, chocolate, a plant and a book."

"What kind of book? Sexy?"

Tezza scowled. "It's a book on how to injure a man without touching him. And once I've read it, I'm going to roll a dice to decide which of you I'll use it on first."

Miquel threw one arm around her shoulders before she could storm off in a huff. "Tezzarina, you're our baby sister. We want you to be happy. If this guy makes you happy and he's got Alba's approval, what's the problem?"

"It's too soon," she whispered. *And he didn't kiss me back.*

"Love is so inconvenient," Alba said, shaking her head.

"He doesn't love me," Tezza protested. "We're just friends."

"For now," Antonio said, grinning. "But any man who brings you coffee gelato can't stay a friend for long, can he?"

Much to Tezza's relief, the conversation shifted to the up-coming holidays and the need for a planned family reunion in the near future, and she slipped away from the table unnoticed.

# Chapter Ten

TEZZA

THE NEXT DAY, AROUND midnight, Tezza unlocked her front door and dragged her duffel and rolling suitcase into the house. She'd left it a disaster area, and she'd need to spend most of the morning working on it. Since it was her house and she was tired just thinking about the cleaning in store for her, it never occurred to her to be quiet about her entrance. She heard a decidedly male noise and looked up. Sam was asleep on her couch, the front curtains shut tightly. He'd thrown a flat sheet over the couch, and that giant denim quilt from his apartment was cast over him haphazardly. *What is he doing here?*

The place was immaculate; her laundry was folded in orderly piles on the coffee table, organized by type. Clean dishes sat dripping in the strainer. More than that, he'd obviously vacuumed and dusted, and when she peeked into the fridge, it was mostly full from three casseroles, six jar salads, and a pot of soup.

*Should I let him sleep? He's probably late enough for work that it doesn't matter . . .* Her suitcase, however, had other feelings on the matter and tipped over with a *klomp* that had him sitting up, rubbing his eyes.

"Hey." He turned on a lamp by the couch.

"Hey," she replied softly.

"You're back."

"Yes." She sat in the modern color-block chair across from the couch to keep her distance—because she wanted to sit on the edge of the couch, pull him toward her by his unshaven chin and kiss him all the way awake. *His sleepy face is so irresistible.*

"What time is it?"

"Around midnight. Aren't you supposed to be at work?"

He shook his head, stretching. "Edward is out of town unexpectedly. They took alternates because I was already committed to watch your place."

"Nice."

"Yeah." He got up the rest of the way, pushing off the quilt, which from the look of it was very heavy. "Can I make you lunch? How was your trip?" Turning on the lights, he went into the kitchen, pulling out pans and plates.

"Sam. Chill."

"But you've been traveling, you're tired. I got to sleep in. Your house is quieter than my apartment. I'm good." He opened the fridge and stuck his head in it to look for something, then stood up suddenly. "Do you want me to go? Are you tired?"

"No. I need to stay up so I'm awake tomorrow night. I'll sleep at five."

His shoulders relaxed. "Cheese toasties okay? It's not healthy, but I can't cook much."

"Who did the salads?"

He shrugged. "Well, I did, but that's just chopping."

"And the casseroles?"

"Grand duchess. She insisted. She said she needs to put that very expensive kitchen to good use or she feels guilty."

Tezza shook her head, smiling despite her fatigue. Abbie was a strange royal, but she couldn't imagine working for anyone else.

"Are you going to move?" He was staring at the counter, slowly grating the cheddar onto the cutting board.

"What?"

"Are you going to move back to Op'Ho'Lonia?"

For a split second, Tezza considered being straight with him. But it wasn't in her nature; she'd always played with her food. And besides, he'd given her nothing since her impulsive kiss but a "did you get there okay?" text when her flight landed. He owed her a little more information about what he was thinking, and he wasn't the kind to come out and just say it.

"I don't know yet."

He was quiet, and she thought for a moment that he was going to actually look at her. He didn't.

"There's a lot of factors to consider," she said solemnly, sidling over to him to press herself against his arm. "A lot of them." If his gaze on her chest was any indication, he liked that, but he was nervous. Putting people at ease was not her specialty; she was far better at frightening the truth out of them.

She took the cheese out of his hand and set it on the counter. "For instance, I own a house here. That's a reason to stay. I have a good job that I like, and my sister is here."

"Any other reasons to stay?" he muttered.

"One or two. One in particular." She flicked her wrist and turned off the smoking cast-iron pan he'd forgotten about, unwilling to break contact with him. "There's some relationships I'd like to pursue now that I'm single."

His head snapped toward her. "Relationships? Plural?"

She nodded soberly, covering his hand with hers. "I've been wanting to get to know my yoga instructor better. She seems nice. We're going to go out for tea next week. And I haven't spent a lot of time outside of work with Addington. I'd like to develop that friendship."

He nodded, visibly relieved.

"And then Alba has a few guys she wants to set me up with."

"What?" His voice was sharper than the grater he was gripping, his knuckles white. "Are you going to go?"

She shrugged with one shoulder. "Can you give me a reason not to?" *Fight, Sam. Fight for us. Don't just let me go. Stand up and take what you want for once instead of going with the flow.*

He sidestepped away from her and went back to making her sandwich, adding avocado and tomato to the cheddar. "I guess not," he said quietly, buttering the top of the bread, balancing the sandwich carefully on a spatula and carrying it across the kitchen to slide it into the still-hot pan.

She pursed her lips. "Not surprising that I've lost my touch after three years, I guess."

He crossed his arms and leaned back against the counter, still holding the spatula.

"What?"

"You must not have liked my kiss."

He shook his head, leaning back to look at the ceiling, as if beseeching an unseen deity for strength. "You haven't lost your touch."

"I must have. There's no other explanation. You didn't like it."

He scowled. "I did like it."

"Nope. Couldn't be."

"Tezza . . . ," he growled. "It's not just about chemistry, is it?"

"You're trying to spare my feelings. I'll save you the trouble. After almost three years of celibacy, I'm sure I'm a terrible kisser and a lousy lay and—"

He slapped her backside lightly with the spatula, and her mouth dropped open.

"You hit me!"

"You were being ridiculous." He showed not an ounce of remorse.

She advanced toward him until they were toe-to-toe. "You *hit* me."

"You goaded me," he said, crossing his arms again. "You were putting words in my mouth. I didn't hurt you." It was true, he hadn't. But she was incensed on principle.

"Samuel Simonson, didn't your mother teach you to use your words?"

He laughed. "You were blatantly ignoring my words."

"Only because they didn't match your actions. Men who've liked my kisses in the past usually wanted more."

He finally looked into her eyes, and she could see him holding back. "How do you know I don't want more?"

"Because we're still talking instead of making out on my couch."

"Maybe I'm just waiting for your sandwich to finish cooking."

She cocked her head. "Are you?"

He smirked as he flipped her sandwich and put down the spatula, moving his hands to her hips, and her heart picked up speed. "Yes. And then I'm going to wait for you to finish eating

. . ." He leaned forward to whisper in her ear. "And then I'm not going to wait anymore."

*Excellent.* Before she could capture any part of him, he moved away, grabbing a plate and depositing her sandwich onto it before he handed it to her.

"But before we do that, we should talk."

"About what?" she asked through her first bite.

"About me. About . . . closeness."

She shuffled to the breakfast bar attached to the kitchen and sat down on a stool, and he followed her.

"Okay."

"It would be different for you and me than it was for you and Rocco. It may take some . . . adjustment."

"Because you're a virgin? I don't care about that." *No sense in being coy.*

"N-no," he stammered. "Not *that*. Because of my neurodiversity." He swallowed hard when she licked the butter off her thumb, and she snickered inwardly. "As I'm sure you've noticed, my perception of sensations is different sometimes. I tried to date in high school. It went badly." He leaned forward. "Things that probably seem very natural to you feel uncomfortable to me."

"Like what?"

"That's the thing; I never know what's going to set me off. It depends on what else happened that day, how frayed my nerves already are. Some days, I may not be able to let you touch me at all."

Tezza thought about this as she ate. For such a good-hearted, generous, handsome man, it didn't seem like that much to give up. She'd never backed down from a challenge.

"I don't mind being creative." She took another large bite. "I can be very determined."

Anxiety and anticipation were fighting over his face, and she chuckled.

"Relax, Sam. It's supposed to be fun."

"Are you done eating?"

She nodded slowly, wiping her greasy hands on a napkin. He held out his hand, and she took it, following him over to the couch. He pulled her onto his lap sideways, and she ran a hand lightly over his biceps. *Woz, I love his arms . . . It feels good to touch him without guilt.*

He flinched. "That's no good." He captured her hand and squeezed, threading their fingers together, then curled them into a stationary position on his chest. She kept the kisses light, teasing, despite his eagerness.

"Can we turn off the kitchen light? The fluorescent is giving me a headache." She wiggled her hand free and flicked a finger toward the kitchen light. She missed. They both grunted. She got it the second time, and she reached to take his face in her hands, but he leaned away from her. "Don't, it's too much. No face touching."

She sat back and sighed through her nose. "You're not even trying."

"I *am* trying," he said, glaring at her. "You're not kissing me hard enough, your shampoo smells terrible, and you keep doing that light touch that makes my skin crawl."

"Am I doing anything right?"

"Your weight on my lap feels good."

She crossed her arms. "That's got nothing to do with technique, petunia. That's just gravity."

He shrugged. "Maybe you've lost your touch after all."

Annoyed, she shoved his chest, and his eyes sparked with interest. "You want it rough, petunia?"

He nodded, pulling her into a hard kiss, squeezing the back of her neck. She let her hands rest on his shoulders and lost herself in the kiss. When he opened his mouth to deeply stroke her tongue with his, her long-neglected sex drive came roaring in, doing donuts, revving its engine. The feeling was heady; she'd forgotten how intoxicating intimacy could be. So intoxicating, in fact, she momentarily forgot who she was with and what he'd told her he needed. Tezza slid her hands to his chest, scratching her fingernails gently over his pecs, and he broke the kiss to push her hands away.

"Tezza!" he yelled. "Seriously, stop!"

Her chest heaving, Tezza shouted back, "Excuse me for enjoying myself! This isn't just about you, you know!"

In the split second before he broke their eye contact, Tezza saw his bitter resignation. He lifted her off his lap and set her gently on the couch.

"You're right. This isn't fair to you."

"Sam, wait." He was already putting on his coat. "Just stop. Let's talk about this."

He snatched up his bag as he opened the front door. "Now you can go pursue those multiple relationships you've been wanting, anyway." He slammed it behind him, and she scrambled across the room to whip it open again.

"There's nobody else, Woz-condemn-it, I was just messing with you. Get back here! Sam!"

Hands jammed deep into his pockets, head down, he was already halfway down the block.

# Chapter Eleven

SAM

AROUND 0500, AS HE was brushing his teeth for bed, Sam got a text.

**Macias: Mandatory training session today before work. 1600 hours.**

**Simonson: I can't be there.**

**Macias: Yes, you will. That's what mandatory means, petunia.**

**Simonson: Stop calling me that.**

**Simonson: Handbook says you're supposed to give 24 hours' notice.**

**Macias: Fine. After work. That's 24.**

**Simonson: Fine.**

**Macias: In case you're wondering, the handbook doesn't say anything about fraternization.**

**Macias: I checked.**

**Simonson: Good. I think Dean's single. You should ask him out.**

**Simonson: Or just kiss him in the middle of a conversation about house sitting.**

**Simonson: I'm sure it'd work better on him than it did with me.**

**Macias: If you drown in that self-pity, I'm not coming in after you.**

**Simonson: You don't think Dean's handsome? I think Terry just broke it off with that dental hygienist. He's got high cheekbones.**

**Simonson: Have you noticed Terry's cheekbones?**

**Macias: I'm not engaging in this with you.**

**Macias: Sleep well.**

**Simonson: You too.**

Sam arrived for work grumpy. After their text exchange, he'd flopped down onto his bed, more than ready for sleep, when he remembered his quilt was still at Tezza's since he'd stormed out. He'd tried to replicate its weight with extra blankets as he'd done at the front during the Brothers' War, but he didn't have enough. He was slamming around the locker room, drawing stares; he didn't care. Simonson trudged upstairs to relieve Dean; Tezza was already there when he arrived outside the family dining room. Since it was a Sunday, the Browards were all eating together. Based on the roar of laughter inside, Simon was cracking everyone up again.

"Hey."

"Hey," she replied, not looking at him.

*Fine. Whatever.*

"Forgot your radio," Dean said. Sam cursed, drawing raised eyebrows from both his coworkers.

"I'll be right back," Sam sighed. "Apologies, sir."

"Nah, I'll get it for you," Dean said. "I go by here on my way out."

"Thanks. Oh—and there's some ibuprofen packets in the break room, can you grab me a few?"

"Sure."

Tezza waited until Dean was out of earshot. "Got a headache?"

"Yes."

"Couldn't sleep without your quilt?"

He scowled. "You make it sound like I'm a toddler who lost my blankie. I'm an adult."

"But that's why, isn't it?"

He ignored her question. If they weren't going to be together, he didn't owe her those kinds of details. They stood in silence until Dean came back with the radio, the medicine, and a glass of water. He watched Sam carefully as he downed two packets.

"You all right, Simonson? I've got alternates if you need to go home."

"I'm fine."

"You look on edge."

"I'm fine, sir."

"Make sure you get some rest tomorrow. Maybe cut out early tonight if you can."

"I've got a mandatory training session at 0500. But I'll go home after that."

Dean cocked his head. "Mandatory training session? I've heard nothing about that." He glanced at Macias, who cleared her throat.

"I've noticed a few deficiencies in Simonson's hand-to-hand approach. I'm going to spend some one-on-one time with him. As one of the security instructors, I can call training when I see fit."

"Uh-huh." Dean grinned. "Well, you two have fun . . . one-on-one."

When Dean was out of earshot again, Sam muttered, "These better be work-related deficiencies, T."

"They are."

"Otherwise, you can just cancel it right now. I don't want to talk about us, because there is no us."

"We'll see about that." A ghost of a smile crossed her face, and he'd just opened his mouth to respond when Abbie and Edward appeared in the doorway. Edward had been drinking and he wagged his eyebrows at them as Abbie put an arm around his waist to stabilize him.

*Lightweight.*

"Abs, look! It's our friends! Hello, friends. Did you have a nice reunion last night?"

"No," Sam replied, just as Tezza said, "Yes."

Edward stopped, swaying a little. "Uh-oh. Why not?"

"You don't have to answer that," Abbie assured Sam, as she pulled on Edward's sleeve to get him moving toward the residence again. "You're being invasive, hon."

"I am not! I care. I care about them. Their love story is just like ours . . ."

Abbie cracked up. "Parker, their story literally could not be more different from ours. Why on earth would you say that?"

"Because he's black like me, and they're falling in love. It's just like us," he said, kissing her cheek, waving his hand, as if shooing away the inconvenient truths getting in the way of his slightly drunk perception. "I'm invested in their getting together and their up-and-down crazy relationship ride . . ."

"Uh-huh," Abbie said, clearly unconvinced. "Let's get you into bed," she cajoled, pulling him down the hall. Edward's eyes twinkled, and he slid a hand over her backside and squeezed.

"Yeah, that's not quite what I meant, but dare to dream, husband." Over her shoulder, she said to the security personnel, "Remember the last time this happened? What is it with him when he's tipsy? Please make a note of this for future events—cut His Majesty off at two drinks lest we expose the grand duchess's backside to public groping."

"But it's such a *nice* backside, darling. I can't help it."

"You resisted when we were dating."

"You've no idea how narrow the margin was, wife. Razor-thin, it was . . ."

They stumbled into the residence, and before long, he could hear Abbie laughing. Apparently, they didn't even make it to the bed; he could hear their heavy breathing and giggling through the door. *It's not fair. It's so damn easy for them. I'd give anything to be able to be with a woman and enjoy being close. But that's never going to happen for me. It would always be a fight, a struggle. She deserves better; she'd have figured that out sooner or later. I'm protecting her. I'm protecting her from disappointment.*

Terry's voice came over the radio. "Kingsguard One, are the royals in for the night?"

"Affirmative."

"I've got a book that the king asked for yesterday; the reference librarian just brought it over. Can I bring it up to you in case he goes back to work tonight?"

"I'll come get it," Sam said quickly.

"Why?" Tezza muttered. "He's buzzed and about to get laid. He's not going back to work tonight."

"You sure?" Terry asked through the radio, not having heard Tezza's comment. "I can run it up."

"No, don't do that. I'll come get it, I haven't made my inspection of this wing tonight yet anyway. They just got home." Without a word to Tezza, he hurried off, relieved that he wouldn't have to listen to any more of his friends' envy-inducing noises.

THE REST OF THE NIGHT passed slowly but uneventfully. At 0500, having seen no sign of Edward, he passed off the book to Dean and headed down to the gym to meet Tezza.

"So what are these so-called deficiencies?" Sam called, entering the low-lit gym, dropping his stuff by the door. "Tezza?"

Before he knew what was happening, Sam felt his legs swept out from under him. Tezza pinned him to the ground on his stomach and whispered, "Lesson one: improve your situational awareness." He felt his wrists go tight together under her muttered incantation.

"Very funny. Now let me up."

She didn't move, and he rocked his hips to the side to throw her off, but without his arms free, he didn't have the leverage. She leaned closer to him, and he waited for the heavy scent of her shampoo to wash over him . . . but it didn't come. *Come to think of it, I didn't smell it all night either.*

"You've never been in love before," she said, her voice husky. "So I wouldn't expect you to understand, but love isn't a feeling; it's a choice. And if you think I'm going to give up over a few bumps in the intimacy road, you're mistaken."

"We're incompatible. Conversation over."

"Compatibility is an achievement, not a prerequisite. And I'm not letting you go until we talk about this."

"Fine. I can lie here all day. The firm pressure you're putting on my back actually feels great. The floor could be a bit softer, but . . ." His voice faltered as Tezza's lips met his neck. "Cheating. That's cheating, T."

"I know," she cooed. She began to suck on his neck, and he bit back a whimper.

"You need to stop," he said firmly. "We're at work. Someone's going to come in here and see us."

"Then I guess we'd better finish our conversation . . ."

"It is finished," he said through gritted teeth as she massaged the stiff muscles in his upper back.

*Woz, that feels good . . .*

"I'm sorry for how I acted last night," Tezza said quietly. "It's been a long time since anyone kissed me like that, and I let myself get carried away." She leaned over and bit his earlobe. "But I can do better. I just need practice."

"You shouldn't have to," he said, still fighting to get free.

"Give me another chance."

"No. We'll just be friends. Friendship is good."

"Oh, but petunia," she whispered, "'more than friends' is so much better. Take it from someone who was very happily married once. It's a state I'm eager to get back to as quickly as possible, and you're my only prospect."

"Broaden your horizons, woman."

Someone cleared his throat from the doorway, and Sam craned his neck to see who it was.

"I apologize," Edward chuckled. "Dean said you were in here. I was going to see if you wanted to go for a run, but I see you're otherwise occupied."

"This is not what it looks like," Sam insisted, but Tezza slapped a hand over his mouth.

"I'm sorry, Your Majesty, but Lieutenant Simonson is doing some hand-to-hand combat training right now."

"That's why his hands are restrained, is it?"

"Yes, sir. He'll be available tomorrow."

Smirking, Edward nudged the gym door shut before continuing down the hall.

"Come over for breakfast tonight," she said, removing her hand from his mouth. "Let's talk."

"Fine. I will come for breakfast. To talk. As a *friend*." With a flick of her wrist, she released his hands, and he rolled his wrists to stretch them out as he dumped her off his back. "Now can we get to work? I want to go home."

As it turned out, he actually did need work on his hand-to-hand skills, and she spent about thirty minutes instructing him and running him through some drills. He was sweaty and spent by the time he got back to the changing room. When he opened his locker, he found his quilt neatly folded on the shelf.

# Chapter Twelve

TEZZA

"WHERE'S YOUR COMPUTER?" It was an odd question to ask while standing at someone's front door, so Tezza let him inside before she answered.

"Next to the couch, I think. Why?"

"I did something for you . . ." He fired it up. "Password?"

"I don't bother. I can always get magical revenge on anyone who steals my identity."

"Fair point. You'll need one for your profile, though."

"My what?"

He grinned at her. "Your dating profile. I signed you up on Another Kind of Magic. It's a site for non-tech magic users to find dates. Isn't that great?"

Tezza reminded her temper that he was young, confused, and in love for the first time. Her temper replied that while this was true, he was deliberately being annoying and therefore deserved to be messed with. She forced herself to take the high road.

"It would be, yes, if I were looking for a non-tech magic user to date. But I'm not interested." She opened the waffle maker and dodged a puff of steam. "How many waffles do you want?"

"You made waffles? That's brilliant. I'll start with four."

Tezza mumbled with bitter envy under her breath about a twenty-two-year-old's metabolism and poured another one onto the iron. He came over and sat at the counter with her computer, and she slid him a plate.

"See? You've got 127 possible matches in our area! I didn't have all your information, so you'll have to help me fill in the gaps."

*Maybe this will be a good way for him to get to know me better...*

"Go ahead and ask."

"Where were you born?"

"Gratacia. It's outside of Brevian." He typed it in carefully as she spelled the town.

"Okay. Do you drink or smoke?"

"I drink socially. I don't smoke. Ever. Also, your waffle is getting cold."

He broke off a bite with the side of his fork. "Do you want to start a family, and if so, when and how many kids do you want?"

Tezza leaned forward, resting her chin on her hands. "I do want kids. Soon. I don't think I care how many. Not too many. And I like the idea of adopting."

His face softened. "Why?"

"I come from a very generous culture. Op'Ho'Lonians see adoption as a way of giving back to the community, of closing the loose ends caused by death and illness and poverty. We don't want our own children to be given away to strangers; we want to care for them ourselves. In a way, they belong to all of us."

He nodded slowly. "Do we have whipped cream?"

She shook her head, smiling. "Something better. Try this." She pulled the custard dessert out of the fridge and brought it around the counter to him. Though she didn't mean to, she got a glimpse of the profile picture he'd uploaded.

"Where did you get that picture of me?" She was riding a horse in the snow, her face soft and contemplative.

He wouldn't even look in her direction, let alone meet her eyes. "That's not important."

"Sam . . ."

He shrugged uncomfortably. "It was in the snow, that one day. That's the only one I took. Promise."

"Woz, you've got it bad, Sam."

He leaned into the computer screen. "I'll be fine, you needn't worry about me. It should be fairly easy to find a man who can give you everything you need. I can at least do that for you." He cleared his throat and went back to the profile. "What are you looking for physically in a match?"

*Screw the high road. It's overrated, anyway.*

"About five foot nine, thick black hair, dark skin, green eyes, strong physique."

He pulled his lips to one side. "That's not going to be easy to find, not many black people have green eyes."

Tezza giggled inwardly. *I might have to be less subtle.*

"What about emotionally, socially? What would you like your mate to be like?"

"As introverted as possible. Very socially awkward. Constantly oversteps in his suggestions and questions."

He typed it in dutifully. "Okay."

"No sense of irony. Easy to mess with. That's important."

"Wait," he said slowly. "Are you describing me?"

"Correction: some sense of irony."

"Oh, Woz preserve me," he said, tapping the "Delete" button forcefully with his index finger. He cleared his throat. "I guess we'll come back to that one. What are three things you're thankful for?"

"Sam's interesting brain. Sam's tender heart. Sam's hot body. In that order."

"I'm not putting that!"

"But that's my answer."

He grunted. "What's your favorite leisure activity?"

She dipped a finger into the custard and licked it off. "Kissing Sam Simonson."

He glared at her. "Really? You aren't going to invest in this whatsoever?"

"I told you I wasn't from the start. Eat your breakfast."

Disgruntled, he stabbed at his food, and his mood immediately shifted when it touched his tongue. "Mmm. This is so good, T. What's in this?" He shoveled more waffle into his mouth and got a little custard at the corner of his lip. Tezza couldn't help herself; a friend would just let you know that it was there and let you deal with it. A girlfriend could be a lot more creative. She reached up toward his mouth, but he leaned away.

"Hold still, petunia. I don't bite."

"You did the other day," he muttered, watching her approaching hand with obvious trepidation. "I still have a mark." She swiped her thumb across his lips, letting her palm rest on his cheek. She could feel him trembling.

"Did you get it?" he mumbled, his eyes never leaving her lips.

"No," she said, leaning closer. "Not yet." She was about to replace her thumb with her lips when her computer started to ring. "Hang on." Turning it more toward herself, she answered.

"Hi, Mama."

"Did you get my package?"

She nodded. "Yes, thank you. I've been missing lime blossom tea." Sam went back to his breakfast, attempting to look like he wasn't listening to their conversation.

"Yes, I saw you drink a lot of it when you were here. Was your house okay?" Tezza took a deep breath. This was an opening. Sam saw it, too, because his eyes went wide, and he started shaking his head even before she got the words out.

"Yes, Sam did a good job watching over things. In fact, he's here now."

"Why did you answer if you were busy?"

"I want you to meet each other." She turned the computer before either of them could object. "Mama, this is Sam Simonson, a close friend of mine." She saw her mother's eyes flicker with recognition at the name. "And Sam, this is my mom, Flor Vivas."

"It's very nice to meet you, Mrs. Vivas."

"Nice to meet you, too, Sam." Her mother gave him a sly grin. "We heard a lot about you on her last visit. Thank you for watching over my baby girl and her house."

"It's my pleasure, ma'am."

His eyes cut to Tezza, but instead of irritation or embarrassment, she saw only pleading. She took pity on him, considering he'd had zero time to prepare for this conversation.

"Mama, I made him your crema capilada for his waffles." Her mother beamed, and Sam blushed so hard that she could see it.

"It's very good," he said, his gaze darting back and forth between the camera and her mother's face on the screen, like he wasn't sure how to make eye contact appropriately.

"Did you broil the top?"

"Yes . . ." She'd used a torch spell rather than dig through the garage to find her actual blow torch. The magic wanted to be used, anyway.

"The secret is a little cinnamon—did you put in the cinnamon, Tezzarina?"

"Of course, Mama," she said, shifting so that they could both be seen on the screen. She wrapped her arms around Sam's chest and rested her chin on his shoulder. If her affectionate hold bothered him, he didn't show it.

He angled his head toward her. "Is that your full name?"

"No," her mom laughed, "just a silly family name. She was always dancing around as a girl, like a ballerina."

In fact, she was playing with a magic her family couldn't see or feel, letting it spin her small body, letting it twirl her like a partner would.

Her father appeared on the screen next to her mother. He wore a serious expression and she felt Sam tense up. She knew now that a gentle touch would not be reassuring to him, so she just squeezed him as hard as she could without making it obvious.

"Hello, Papa. This is Sam."

"Hello, Mr. Vivas." He gave the imposing older man on the screen a weak wave.

"Hello, *Sam*." He said his name like a warning, but Tezza knew he was teasing. He'd always loved freaking out her boyfriends. Sam's image on the screen told her he was sweating.

"I assure you, sir, I have nothing but honorable intentions toward your daughter."

"Not entirely honorable, I hope," her father boomed. "I want more grandkids, *Sam*."

Tezza smothered her laughter on his shoulder, but it was still infectious, and Sam laughed, too. *Should I throw him under the bus?*

"Papa, it's a bit early to be talking about kids. Sam was just trying to set me up with a stranger on a dating site."

"Oh, Samuel . . ." Her mother's voice was thick with withering disappointment. "Why would you do this thing? You don't like our Tezza?"

"Of, of course I do," he stammered. "I like her a lot. I want her to be happy with someone well-suited to her . . . someone who can give her everything she needs."

Her mother went on as if he hadn't responded. "All her time with us, everyone said she made a terrible widow. Terrible. She wears the black, yes, she cries, but her face is like the full moon every time she talks about you. How can you take that from her?"

"I wasn't—I mean, I'm not . . ."

"A stranger?" Her father also ignored Sam's protests and shook his head gravely. "No, no, Sam. *You* will take her out. We don't want strangers with her. She's a good girl." Tezza alternated between wondering what they'd think about her tying Sam up and wondering if her dad would ever realize she was thirty years old.

"No offense, sir, but your 'girl' could kick my butt any day of the week. She doesn't need protection from strangers."

"Not her physical safety, no," Mr. Vivas replied, looking at him over the top of his reading glasses. "But her heart, Sam. Who will protect her heart?"

Sam stared at the screen, saying nothing, and for once, she wasn't sure what was happening in his head. The extended silence was starting to make Tezza uncomfortable; her father was clearly expecting an actual answer. Then she felt a tug on her elbow. He was pulling her in front of him to look at her, and he took her face in his hands.

"I will," he said softly. "I'll protect her heart."

"That's right. Or you'll answer to me," her father said, and her mother gave a watery sigh.

"Bye, Mama, bye, Papa," Tezza said, without looking at the screen. "Love you." She closed the laptop over her mother's objections.

"I can't believe I didn't think of that. He's right. You can't go out with just anyone. He might break your heart." He suddenly pulled her into a tight hug, and she could feel him tug at the end of her long ponytail, then lift it.

"Did you change your shampoo?"

"Yes."

"For me?"

"You said it smelled terrible."

"It does. But I shouldn't have said anything. It's your body, it can smell like whatever you want it to smell like . . ."

"Is this one better?" She'd gone out that night, despite her exhaustion, and found one that was as inoffensive as possible.

He nodded, rubbing his stubbly cheek against her soft one. "Much better."

"Then I'll throw the other one away."

"That's impractical."

"So it was practical for you to come all the way over here to have breakfast?"

He shook his head, letting his hands rest in the curve of her lower back.

"And was it practical for me to go out just to buy cream so I could make you my mother's famous waffle topping?"

He shook his head again.

"There are more stars than I need to navigate by, but they still take my breath away on a clear night. There's more flowers than I can pick in a field, but I still stop to watch them sway in the wind. Love, Sam. Love is often impractical."

He said nothing as they stood close, and she breathed him in for a few moments.

Sam cleared his throat softly. "Maybe you could use your old shampoo on days when you're not going to see me."

She grinned. "What if I want to see you every day?"

"Do you?" he asked, a little breathless. She nodded. "Why?"

"Why?" She laughed. "Because I like you, petunia."

His answering grin was teasing. "But we're not friends, Macias. You told me so." She laughed again. "Since when do you like me?"

"Since you blushed taking your pants off outside my flooding bathroom. I saw what was happening there."

"That's naughty, Macias."

She drew back to see him better. "Sam, I know I've been pushing you . . ."

"Hounding is more like it."

She snickered, then sobered. "But if we do this, it has to be because you want to, not because you think it's what I need. Your whole life is about what other people need. But you are allowed to need things, too."

"I do need things," he said, his eyes heating, "very specific things."

She swatted his shoulder. "But I'm a good girl," she said, playfully mimicking her father's accent. "Good girls don't like to be kissed, do they?"

"I know one who does," he said, brushing her cheek with his nose. "She likes it a lot."

"You're such a tease," Tezza whispered, squeezing his arms, and she heard him chuckle. He cleared his throat and gave her what she could only assume was intended to be a stern look.

"This is on a trial basis," he said. "I'm not promising anything."

"Right," she said, feigning solemnity, nodding.

"It's going to be bumpy," he murmured, kissing just below her ear.

"Uh-huh," she breathed, tipping her head back to give him better access.

"Woz, you're pretty," he murmured against her neck. "Gorgeous, really."

"Mm-hmm." She started backing toward the couch and he followed.

"And smart. And funny. And tough."

"Yes."

"Woz, it's going to break my heart when this doesn't work out."

"Quiet," she laughed, bringing his lips back up to hers. As he was rather good at following directions, neither of them said anything for quite a while after that.

# Chapter Thirteen

TEZZA

"READY FOR OUR FIRST official date?" he asked, rubbing his hands together.

"Yes. Where are we going?"

"It's a surprise."

"I hate surprises."

Sam rolled his eyes at her. "But it's the good kind of surprise, like on your birthday, not the nasty kind like when you think you're eating yogurt and it's really mayonnaise."

Tezza's lip curled in disgust. "Has that happened to you?"

"Oh, no. I avoid wobbliness of all varieties in my food. Yogurt is out of the question for me. I don't eat yogurt."

She snickered, and he slid his fingers between hers as they exited the castle grounds. "No gelatin, then?"

"Woz no. Disgusting."

"Sour cream?"

He considered this. "I put that in the same category as your delicious crema stuff that you made for me. It has enough density to be palatable, and it's usually mixed with something. But just taking a spoon and digging into pudding? No. I don't think so."

Tezza looked down at their interlocked fingers, thinking. It felt different being connected to someone again, being someone else's "and." Not a bad different, just different. It would take some to get used to. An unexpected wave of grief hit her, and she let it roll over her, then accepted the peace that came next. She was starting to recognize a pattern: if she fought the grief, it stayed. But if she let it come, welcomed it even, then it rolled through without incident, like an invading army. Let it conquer, even briefly, and it would not destroy. Let it in, and it would let itself out.

She looked at Sam, who was watching the sidewalk, smiling. "What are you grinning about?"

"I'm with you."

"You stood next to me all night, petunia."

"Not like this." He squeezed her hand, and her heart echoed it. She didn't go in for PDA, but if she did, that would've earned him a kiss for sure.

"You're a hand-holder, huh?"

"Don't know. Never tried it, really. It seems all right." He lifted their joined hands, examining them closer, drawing a smile out of her. He kissed the back of her hand with a smile, then let them drop again. They turned the corner into an alley, and Sam knocked on a nondescript gray door with no outside handle.

"This isn't a restaurant."

"Nope."

The door opened, and an older white man with a big belly stood smiling at them. Sam dropped her hand and ushered her inside the darkened warehouse.

"Morning, Samuel." He kept his thumbs hooked into his suspenders as he led them into the big room.

"Hi, Uncle Frank. Uncle Frank, this is my girlfriend, Tezza Macias."

He stopped and pivoted slowly at that. "Girlfriend? Woo, hoo-hoo . . . Do your mum and dad know about her? I think Serena would've put that on the front page of the family newsletter . . ."

"Lots of people have girlfriends. It's not newsworthy." He kept walking past the man, ignoring his attempt to continue the conversation.

"Sure," the man chuckled, "sure, Sam. Lots of people, but not you." Tezza bristled at the insinuation, and he hurried to correct himself. "At least, not until now. I'm glad to see it, don't get me wrong, I'm just . . . surprised. Usually when you say you're bringing someone, it's the joker or the stone-faced fella."

"This is our first official date, and it's on a trial basis. I would appreciate it if you didn't mention her to my parents."

Uncle Frank guffawed at that, and Sam turned to her with a pained expression that made Tezza fight to hold in a smile.

"Come on," he said, pushing them both into the hallway. "Let's get to the fun part. Tezza's hungry."

"Can she not speak for herself, young nephew?"

Tezza cleared her throat and stuck out her hand. "Nice to meet you, Frank."

"Likewise, young lady. You've got a firm grip there. You're willing to go into a strange warehouse with this character? Are you the trusting sort?"

Now Sam was the one laughing out loud, and she loved the sound. She couldn't remember the last time she'd heard him really burst out loud like that.

"I can usually handle myself in unfamiliar situations, sir."

"She's my partner. I would never knowingly put her in danger," Sam added. He was rubbing his hands together again.

*What's he doing?*

"You starting a fire there?" she asked, and he just smiled cryptically. Uncle Frank led them up a metal staircase, flipping on lights as he went, and then unlocked a room at the top of the stairs. It was full of weapons. *Nice* weapons. She started to pick up a crossbow with a curved grip unlike any she'd ever seen before, but Sam handed her a pair of shatterproof glasses.

"Safety first."

She dutifully donned the glasses and a reinforced vest that he held out for her like a jacket.

"All right, now you can dig in. Uncle Frank designs and imports weapons. I asked him if we could come play with his toys. This is the showroom; the range is down below. Pick what you want to try first."

Now Tezza was the one rubbing her hands together; at least, she was on the inside. She selected the crossbow she'd seen first, a longbow with a unique eccentric wheel, and a set of throwing knives with an interesting diamond-shaped blade. As they made their way down, she noticed Sam had chosen all throwing knives. She'd noticed that he favored knives when he armed himself around the castle, but she'd never taken the time to look at them. Uncle Frank opened up the range and Tezza frowned.

"There's no targets."

"I know." Sam grinned. "You're going to provide the targets."

She crossed her arms. "That sounds like work. This is a date. Dates are for fun."

He drew her forward by her elbows. "You really don't want to? I just wanted to see what you could do. You're so good with magic . . ." His hands drifted to her back, and he rubbed in light circles. "Please? You supply my targets, and I'll go get the automatic ones for yours . . ."

"I never pegged you for a flatterer, Simonson." She heard Uncle Frank chuckle. "Fine. But I get to go first."

"Deal." He jogged over to set up the electronic targets, which looked like fuzzy blue circles bouncing around a large rectangle, much like the screensaver on her TV. She picked up the knives first, weighing one in her hand, holding it by the handle.

"You'll want to use a pinch grip for those," Sam said, his mind occupied by the setup.

"You sound very sure of yourself."

Sam continued to program the targets, but he grinned.

"How often do you come here?"

He shrugged. "Once or twice a month."

"Not lately, young man; you've been here weekly. I knew you weren't just brushing up on your skills; no one throws a knife like that without some unexpressed affection aggression."

Sam rolled his eyes. "Uncle Frank wants to retire. He's trying to convince me to take over the business."

"And here I thought you were missing all those hints I've been dropping," Frank called from his stool in the corner.

"That would be impossible," Sam called back. "You have no subtlety."

"Look who's talking!"

"Whatever, Frank." He glanced at Tezza quickly. "You ready?"

She nodded and he started the targets moving. Their movement was fairly predictable, but every so often, they would bounce or ricochet off an unseen obstacle or edge. She lifted her hand and whipped the three knives toward the targets. She missed the first two and barely caught the edge of the third one. Tezza cursed quietly, and Sam laughed as he trotted to collect her knives for her.

"Try again, tough girl."

She rallied the magic to her this time, kept her touch light on the handles. *Is this cheating? Only sort of.* She'd use magic if she were defending the royals, she reasoned, therefore the augmentation was appropriate. The first one she speared through the middle, the second one nicked the edge, and the third one missed completely.

"Ready to try it my way?" Sam smirked and Tezza smacked him on the arm. "Hey," he laughed, "I'm just trying to help. Use your words."

"Fine. Show me your way."

"I don't think that would be a very . . ."

"Excuses," Tezza sniffed.

Sam picked up the first knife by the back of the blade and threw all three dead center. "As I was saying," he continued, straightening the remaining weaponry on the table, "I don't think my demonstration is a fair comparison, because I've practiced a lot with this set and I have strong wrists. But you're using a hammer throw instead of a pinch grip. So just turn them over and your speed and accuracy will improve."

That unassuming, efficient authority—that was her catnip. She wanted to pick up a knife, cut all his clothes off and show him the advantages of dating a woman who'd been married before. But he hadn't looked at her face, so he was missing all the body language she was giving him.

"Frank, don't you have some work to do upstairs?" she said. Sam paused mid-pull where he was retrieving the knife from the wall and turned to look at her, then at Frank, his shoulders tense.

"As a matter of fact, young lady, I do. I believe I'll just wander up and do some . . . work." He chuckled as he shuffled toward the door. "I'll be back in a few minutes, so don't get carried away. That table's for *weapons*."

Sam set the knives down and turned to lean against the table, bracing his arms behind him on the edge, his head almost to his chest. "I'm sorry."

"Sorry for what?" She came around to the other side and stood in front of him with her arms crossed for . . . reasons. *Sam's trying to have an emotional discussion and doesn't need me pawing at him right now* reasons.

"For whatever I did wrong. I'm sorry if I caused you embarrassment or if you felt I instructed you in a way that was . . ."

She slipped her arms around his waist and hugged him tight, listening to his heart beating madly. "You didn't do anything wrong, Sam."

He pressed his nose into her hair and sighed, his arms coming around her. "I didn't?"

"Nope."

"Are you certain? Because often when people send away spectators, it's because I'm going to get yelled at."

"That's not the only reason to get rid of spectators, petunia." Her hands were beginning to wander on their own, and she told her body to settle the Jersey down. It ignored her.

"Oh . . ." She heard the recognition in his voice. "Oh. You liked my demonstration?"

She nodded slowly, and her hungry lips met his neck where his beard started. *Whoops. Just slipped right up there. How'd that happen?*

"And when Frank said not to get carried away, he meant . . . oh."

"Kiss now. Talk later," Tezza muttered, at the end of her patience, sliding off his safety glasses. He finally engaged then, laughing a little, leaning into her more fully. She felt the heat of his embarrassment under her fingers as she rubbed the rough stubble on his cheeks.

"Not my face," he reminded her gently, as he caught her hands and intertwined them behind her back so he was still holding her. Bent slightly backwards, her center of gravity behind her, it felt like she was falling in every sense possible—hopelessly, contentedly falling for this incredible man who always assumed he was screwing up.

"You're good with knives," she whispered between kisses, his breath still warming her lips. "You're good at a lot of things. I wish you understood that."

He blushed again. "I . . ."

"And quit assuming I'm mad at you. When I'm mad, you'll know."

"Okay," he said. "Will you try the pinch grip now?"

"How could I not after your hot demonstration?"

"Hot?" Sam popped an eyebrow. "Not sure about that . . ."

"Trust me, petunia. Hot."

He shrugged, grinning. "You're the expert."

"On hot, maybe. Not on knives. That's you, apparently."

"I just have more practice."

"You're too modest. Now I know why they really wanted you in Op'Ho'Lonia. Better at tracking? I don't think so." She reached behind him to pick up the knives, grasping them by the unsharpened side of the blade. It felt strange, but almost everything today had. Tezza turned, aimed, and fired the knife at the circle. She claimed the first one, then the second, then the third.

"Well done! Now try this set, you'll like it better."

Uncle Frank wandered back in while she tried the second set, which she did like much better. Sam went over to talk to him while she tried out the crossbow and the longbow, both of which ended up being fun but nothing special.

"Here." Sam thrust the black leather carrying case for her favorite set of knives toward her. "They're yours."

"What?"

"I bought them for you. I get an employee discount when I work the warehouse sales. There's one coming up next week, but Uncle Frank let me have them now."

She clutched them to her chest the way some women might clutch a bouquet of long-stemmed roses. "You didn't have to . . ."

He shut her up with a kiss that made her tingle all the way down to her toes, and she quite forgot that Uncle Frank was even in the room.

"Let's go get you some dinner." He put an arm around her waist and kissed her temple like he couldn't help himself as he led her toward the hallway.

"Dinner?" Frank asked. "It's 6:30 a.m."

"Bye, Uncle Frank."

"See you next week, young man."

"Yep," Sam called over their shoulders.

"And you're taking over my business next year!"

"I'll think about it."

It wasn't until after Sam had walked her home that she realized she hadn't given him what he'd asked for; he'd never taken his turn.

# Chapter Fourteen

SAM

**TEZZA: IT'S MY TURN to plan a date.**

    **Sam: Why does that frighten me?**

    **Tezza: Because you're a smart man.**

    **Sam: Whatever it is, I'm still paying. Not negotiable.**

    **Tezza: We can go dutch. Skydiving is expensive.**

    **Sam: Um, I'm not going skydiving.**

    **Tezza: Meet me at the palace airfield at 1600 hours.**

    **Sam: Seriously, T. I'm not going skydiving.**

    **Sam: What are we really doing?**

    **Tezza: You'll see. Bring throwing knives.**

    **Sam: Can't wait.**

    **Tezza: Sarcasm?**

    **Sam: No! Of course not.**

    **Sam: Sleep well.**

    **Tezza: You too.**

Sam rubbed the handkerchief in his pocket as he entered the castle grounds. He quickly took his backpack to his locker then went to find his crazy girlfriend. His crazy girlfriend, who purported to hate PDA, then made out with him practically in front of his uncle. His crazy girlfriend, who never missed an opportunity to make him nervous. Not that it was hard—he wanted this relationship to work so bad, it was bordering on unhealthy. Last night, he'd had a nightmare that she'd broken up with him by text message because he was "not my type after all," but then he still had to go to work and stand next to her all night. He woke up a sweaty mess.

So when he showed up at the airfield, he was already a little on edge. He'd stuck his favorite set of knives in his back pocket, just in case she wasn't kidding. He'd designed them himself a few summers ago, and they were one of Uncle Frank's best sellers. He gave him a cut of each set he sold, even though Sam had urged him not to. It was money he now referred to as "ring money" in his head. Yeah, a little unhealthy . . . but he was going to lock this down if it killed him. A woman this amazing would not slip through his fingers. He would just keep spoiling her, keep making her laugh, keep giving her whatever she needed until he was indispensable.

She wasn't in the flight planning office. He pulled out his phone.

**Sam: Where are you?**

**Tezza: Just getting on my parachute.**

**Sam: Very funny.**

**Tezza: Hangar 4. Last one on the right.**

The aircraft-sized door was closed, so he peeked his head in through the pedestrian door. It was surprisingly warm inside. *Please be kidding about skydiving . . .* Tezza stood with her back to the door, and he admired the view of her from behind for a moment before he touched her elbow. She jumped.

"Woz, you're quiet. Hi."

"Hi."

She leaned in for a kiss, but he turned his head. "We're at work, T."

She crossed her arms. "We're not on the clock, and we're alone." His stomach churned. He couldn't mix personal with professional quite so easily.

"But we're on the grounds. There's cameras everywhere. It's work." Some movement overhead caught his eye, and Sam looked up. *Birds.* They were every size and shape, fantastic reds and oranges and blues, just like the furnishings of her house. He was still staring, slack jawed, when she reached into his back pocket and took his knives.

"You asked for targets. So here you go."

"Do you know," he said, still gawking at the magic apparitions that flapped and floated overhead, "how much money Frank's clients would pay for something like this?"

"Does that mean you like it?"

"How long did this take you?"

"Does that matter?"

He pivoted to look at her. *Bags under her eyes, posture a little slumped, clothes wrinkled.*

"Did you sleep today?"

She handed him back his knives. "They should come back to the case within a minute or two after being thrown, so if you miss, don't worry about it. The birds you hit will drop to the ground, obviously."

"Tezza," he growled. "Tell me you didn't stay up all night doing this."

"I didn't stay up all night doing this."

He put a hand on his hip. "Because you technically stayed up all *day* doing this, right?"

She gave him a small grin, then gestured over her shoulder. "I'm gonna go nap in the locker rooms. I'll see you at 1700." She shuffled toward the exit.

"Hey!" he yelled at her back. "How is this a date if you're leaving?"

"Sam, I need sleep. I won't be able to work without it. Just enjoy."

He took a few long strides to catch up with her and grabbed her elbow to whip her back around to face him. "You shouldn't have gone to all this work just for me, I didn't realize the cost of what I was asking for. I just wanted a little more of a challenge than the floating circles. You shouldn't have done this."

"Are you upset with me?" *Raised volume, eyes wide, eyebrows high, posture rigid. Angry with a side of disbelief.*

"No, no," he said quickly. *Just terrified that I'm asking for too much.*

She pushed at his chest. "Yes, you are. You're angry. Just say it."

Sam balled his fists, but it wasn't helping him bail the conflicted feelings flooding his insides. He jammed his hands into his pockets. "No. I'm not. You just misunderstood what I wanted. It was a misunderstanding. I'm sorry. It was selfish of me to ask; I didn't mean to take so much of your time."

Tezza looked like she'd been slapped. A crack like thunder reverberated in the hangar, and he looked up to see a cloud of feathers; the birds had exploded. "Take so much of my time?" She jabbed him in the chest with one finger, and he flinched as he forced his gaze back down to her. "You didn't take anything, you jackass; *I gave it to you*. I gave it to you because there's nothing I wouldn't give you." She shoved him, and he stumbled backwards, fighting to stay calm. "And until you understand that I need to express my love just as much as you do, this isn't going to work."

"Your . . . your love?" It was a good thing she'd gotten the pushing out of her system already, because if she'd pushed him again, he'd have tipped right over and cracked his head on the concrete floor.

"Yes, Sam!" she shouted. "My love! What do you think we're doing here?"

"It was on a trial basis," he murmured, distraught, yet still distracted by the slow-motion rain of feathers. *Should I be afraid right now?*

"No, *you* were on a trial basis. Not me." She snatched her bag off a chair. "Call me when you're ready to commit." *She's leaving. She's leaving.*

"Where are you going? Wait. Tezza, please. I'm sorry."

"Apology not accepted," she snapped. The slamming door echoed in the empty hangar. It might as well have been a cell door: he was officially in relationship jail. Sam sat down hard on the concrete floor, his head in his hands. He didn't move until his phone buzzed with a text message.

**Bluffton Security Central Dispatch: You were due to report for work at 1700 hours. Do you need a replacement?**

*Shit.* It was already 1710, and he still had to get across the grounds back to the palace.

**Sam: Sorry. On my way.**

*On my way to play out my nightmare in real life.* He hurried to the royals' residence, dodging other employees on the stairs, ignoring the odd looks he was getting for running through the palace.

"Sorry, sorry," he panted.

Dean scowled at him. "You're late."

"I know, I'm sorry." He'd forgotten his radio. *Shit*.

"Is everything all right, Simonson?" Georgie asked, her eyes narrowed.

"Yes, everything is—where's Tezza?"

"Macias went home sick. They're finding me a replacement."

*Shit infinity. Shit to the nth degree. Shit googleplex.*

"She looked awful," Dean added. "You don't look so great yourself, Simonson."

"I'm fine. Sorry again. I'll take over now."

"I'll bring you up a radio," Dean said, as he started down the long hall.

"Thank you, sir."

He could feel Addington's eyes on him as he struggled to regain his composure and a normal breathing pattern, but he didn't look at her.

A white man Sam didn't recognize was approaching the residence, with Dean right behind him, so Sam assumed they were together and he waved him through.

"Hey, whoa." Georgie shot out a hand to stop the man. "Aren't you going to frisk him?"

"Oh. Right." Sam patted the man down, but found nothing suspicious. He opened the door for the man.

"Did you get his ID?" Dean asked, glaring.

"No, I . . . Sir, may I see some ID?"

As soon as the ID was recorded and checked, Sam closed the door to find his supervisor staring at him.

"Why are you acting like it's your first day on the job, Simonson?"

Shame had his chin dropping to his chest. "I'm sorry, sir. I'm fine. Really."

"No, you're not," Georgie said. "It's pretty obvious why, too."

Dean crossed his arms. "Maybe you picked up the same bug Macias has. Go home."

"No," Sam said forcefully. "I'm not sick. I'm here to work."

"You may be, but your mind's not." Dean stepped closer and lowered his voice. "Don't make me involve anyone else in this. Go home and get your head straight. We'll see you Monday night."

Sam hesitantly headed back down the hall, looking over his shoulder. Sullenly, he gathered his things and went back to his apartment.

## TEZZA

IT WAS POURING OUTSIDE, the kind of midsummer rain that spoils picnic plans and prompts newspaper umbrellas. She felt the vibrations from the thunder through the hardwood as she pressed herself away from the floor into another push-up. It was the perfect weather for feeling upset. Two days, and she'd heard nothing from him. *Two days.* How had she gotten so attached to him in just a few months? How did he have this kind of power over her?

There was a knock. Her heart seized. The tall, dark shadow was about the right size. She scrambled to answer the door, then took a deep breath to try to play it cool. He stood there, water cascading out of her overflowing gutters behind him.

"What kind of commitment do you want?" Sam asked over the roar of the rain. He looked like he was going to throw up.

She pulled one arm behind her back with the other to keep from folding them across her middle. "I don't know. But I don't want you to have an easy out. Because it wouldn't be easy for me."

"Me either." He lifted his hands, as if to rest them on her hips, but stopped himself, tucking them under his armpits. "I'm not ready to get engaged."

"Fine. But stop acting like this"—she gestured between them—"can be undone at a moment's notice."

Sam nodded slowly. "I just want you to have everything you need . . ."

"And if I want the same for you?" She gentled her voice. "I've lost track of all the things you've done for me. Yet I tried to do something for you—something you even asked me for—and you freaked. Why is that, Sam?"

He shrugged with one shoulder, staring at her porch light. "I'm too much."

"What does that mean?"

"I don't want my limits to be a burden. I don't want you to resent me."

"And you think I'll resent your needs?"

"You might." It was hard to hear him—he said it so softly, eyes still fixed on the stupid porch light. "You don't know the full extent yet. I was trying to . . . to ease you into it. Give you more reasons to stay first."

"Don't. Give it to me. All of it. Let me decide if it's too much."

He finally gave her his soft green gaze. "May I come in?"

She moved aside, and they stood together in the entryway.

"I've been doing a lot of thinking these last two days. About us. About my past relationships. About the future. About my uncle's business." He shifted his weight back and forth between his feet. "And I think I haven't agreed to take it over for the same reason I couldn't accept your gesture on our last date. It's just hard to believe that you'd want to do that for me . . . Giving to you feels right, natural. Getting the same treatment from you feels uncomfortable. I almost feel like I tricked you, like I manipulated you into it somehow."

"Sam. Look at me." She pointed to herself. "Do I look like someone who's easily manipulated?"

One corner of his mouth turned up. "No."

"If you're not sure, we could wrestle again."

"No, thank you." He sighed, running a hand over his head. "I'm new at this; I don't know how it all works. I don't want to take advantage of you, T."

"You're not. My gestures, big or small, come from my heart. And if I need space or distance, I'll ask for it. Trust me." She sighed, touching her ponytail, smoothing it down. "I've had time to think, too. I've been . . . rushing things with you. Maybe to avoid dealing with my grief over Rocco." Tezza turned toward the window and tried to blink back her tears.

"Have you thought about seeing a counselor?"

She growled, crossing her arms over her chest. "All they want to do is talk."

In her peripheral vision, she could see him covering his mouth with one hand, nodding, and she knew he was trying not to laugh. Tezza smacked him on the arm with the back of her hand, then noticed for the first time how soaked he was; he was shaking. "You're drenched. Are you cold?"

He nodded.

"Take off your shirt. Why aren't you wearing a coat?"

"I've been a little distracted the last few days." He paused. "I don't think any of your shirts will fit me." Tezza jogged down the hall to grab a towel and the shirt she'd bought him. She pushed both at him, then moved to fill the teakettle. A cold Orangie would want tea.

"What's this?"

"That's a towel, petunia." He stripped off his sopping shirt, revealing his hard chest, and Tezza could've sworn that the windows in the kitchen began to fog up.

He scowled. "I meant the shirt. Where did it come from?"

"I went to a D-Descareti tailor."

"Why?"

"T-to get you a shirt with flat seams."

"Why are you stuttering? I've never heard you stutter before."

*I never have. But now your beautiful, bare brown chest is in front of me, and apparently, my mouth can't take it.*

She shrugged one shoulder and turned so that he wouldn't see her face, but it was too late. She felt his heat at her back, just shy of touching her.

"You know," he said, his voice dropping to a deeper register, "Abbie's been helping me improve at reading body language, too."

She tried to keep her tone casual. "Really?" One word was all she could get out.

He nodded slowly, the tip of his nose caressing her cheek. "Particularly attraction nonverbals."

Tezza tried to change the subject. "The flat seams should be more comfortable on your skin."

"Mmm. Did you know your cheeks are flushed?"

*Does he know that he's flirting with me? Or is he just being curious?* Either could be true with Sam. "I was just exercising."

"And your respiration is increased." He laid his strong hands lightly on her hips, his sandpaper thumbs brushing just above the waistband on her skin.

*Oh. Yeah, he's starting something.* "Like I said. Exercising."

"Hmm." He tipped her chin toward him until they were looking into each other's eyes. "And your pupils are dilated," he whispered. "Is that from exercising, too?"

"No," Tezza whispered back.

He dropped the confident act. "Even when you're mad at me?"

"Even then." She licked her dry lips. "P-put the shirt on. Please."

Chuckling, he complied, covering up his beautiful body, despite the silent, disappointed blubbering of her own body, which apparently had a mind of its own and wanted Sam. She couldn't blame it. She shook her head, trying to get back on track with their conversation.

"It comes down to this: you think you're a nuisance, because you're socially awkward and miss nonverbal cues and ask inappropriately intimate questions. But Sam, that's what makes you Sam. You're compensating unnecessarily. Stop it. Please."

"I'll try. For your sake."

"No!" she laughed. "For *your sake*. That's the point."

"Right." He grinned sheepishly. "I'll try, for my own sake."

"Good."

"And will you go to a counselor? For your sake?"

She thought hard. She couldn't promise something she wouldn't do. "I'll try it once. Will you go with me?"

"If you want me to. Though I think my awkwardness will likely make the whole situation more uncomfortable . . ."

Tezza shook her head. "All you have to do is hold my hand."

"I can do that." He took both her hands in his.

"I know. That's one reason I love you." She rested her head on his chest. "I meant what I said. I do love you, at least a little bit."

"I love you at least a little bit, too." He bit his bottom lip. "I wasn't intending to let you say it before me. I was going to give us a few more dates first. But you beat me to it in typical fashion. I wanted to say it back in the hangar, but I was very overwhelmed and I regret now that I—"

Tezza kissed him. She kept her hands intertwined with his, pulling him against her body. *No face touching, no light touch. Stay focused.*

"Am I ever going to get to finish a speech?" he asked, scowling.

She shook her head, grinning, and he grinned back.

# Chapter Fifteen

TEZZA

*HE HAS NO IDEA WHAT he's doing to me,* Tezza thought. Oh, he knew what he was doing; after just a few months together, the man was a quick learner. He was lavishing her with the exact kind of kisses she craved; slow, deep, adoring. She knew he was doing it intentionally, because he'd stopped all her attempts at reciprocation, even pinning her hands under her legs to keep her from touching him lightly by accident so he wouldn't be annoyed or distracted. She wasn't used to beating back her response to a man's closeness anymore—married women don't need to, after all. Rocco had certainly encouraged and enjoyed her eagerness. It was getting easier to think about him . . . that Rocco was gone. All that dumb talking had helped a little bit. Time was filing off the sharpest edges of grief, but it still cut her sometimes, made her bleed. He held her then, too.

Sam cradled her face in both his hands, brushing his thumb along her jaw. It was possessive and tender, and it was pushing all her buttons in a delightfully problematic way. But when he reached up and pulled the tie out of her hair to let it fall around her shoulders, she wrenched her shaking hands out and pressed herself away from him.

"What's wrong?" he asked, his voice thick, his gaze a little kiss-drunk.

*What's wrong? You might as well have been undressing me just now.*

He drew his eyebrows into a deep V. "What's that face mean, love? I thought you liked it like this." She couldn't keep a laugh from bubbling out.

"Yes, I do like it like this, *very much*."

He grinned, clearly pleased with himself, and moved toward her again, but she held him away, much to her body's chagrin.

"But . . ."

He lifted one eyebrow. "But?"

"But that was my 'walk to the bedroom or I'll carry you there' face."

He rubbed the back of his neck as he laughed softly. "Ah. I see."

"Now," she went on, "if you want to get in a blimp and take a quick trip to the Land of Lust . . ."

He blinked. "You want to elope in Descaret?"

She shrugged. "I'm game if you are."

"Tezza," he sighed. "I know you're a practical woman . . ." He smoothed her hair away from her face. "And believe me, it's one of your best traits, but we've only been dating a few months."

"Okay, sugarlump."

He grimaced. "Is that better than 'petunia'? I don't know . . ."

"That's what my mother calls my father," Tezza said, nuzzling his neck. "And my yaya called my yayo."

"Are those your grandparents?"

She nodded, inhaling deeply. Sam smelled like nothing but himself. She pressed closer.

"Did you use that name for Rocco?"

She stopped to think. Had she? Her twenties had been marked by a rejection of her home culture that she just couldn't maintain in her thirties. Traditions and customs seemed so important these days, in a foreign country, in a way they hadn't at home. Perhaps it was a way of finding her community. "No. I didn't."

He swallowed hard. "I'm sorry, that was . . . Forgive me. I shouldn't have pried."

"I don't mind," she whispered, bringing their foreheads together. "Ask me anything."

"Was he good in bed?"

Her heart broke a little, looking into his vulnerable eyes, but she nodded.

"Thank you for not lying to me," he said, looking away. She wanted to gently push his face back toward hers, but she let him take some emotional distance.

"But not at first."

He turned back on his own. "Really?"

"Of course. Neither was I. But we loved each other. We trusted each other. I asked him not to lick me. He asked me not to moan so loudly in his ear." She grinned at Sam's blush.

"I knew you'd be loud," he whispered, and she giggled as she brought their lips back together for a brief, cherishing kiss, the kind meant to remind him that every bit of this was okay.

SAM

SAM WAS FIGHTING HIS senses hard. Edward had invited them all over, and since it was Saturday, Sam could actually go.

He hadn't hung out with his friends in so long, he wanted to stay, to participate. But he found himself drawing away, sitting on the farthest edge of the couch. They were crunching chips. The volume was too loud on the video game, his app said it was 79 decibels. Way too loud. He'd worn the wrong shirt; it was new, hadn't been washed enough yet, even though it said it was 100 percent cotton. Even the flashing on the screen grated, his eyes felt accosted.

"Sorry I'm late," Tezza said to no one in particular as she walked in. She stopped abruptly in front of Sam. "What's wrong?"

He avoided her gaze. "Nothing."

"Don't bullshit me, Simonson," she warned. "I know nothing, and this isn't it."

He ran a hand over his face. "Lay off, T. I just had a long day."

She seemed to hesitate for a moment, then went around the back of the couch to stand behind him. He felt her strong hands begin kneading his shoulders.

"No offense, but I'm not in the mood . . ." That's when he felt the magic stirring around him. "Is that you?" he muttered, and she hummed her affirmation. "What're you doing?"

"Helping." The magic trickled down his spine like cool water, flowing across his overexcited nerves, flushing out the static. The music's volume reduced, losing no clarity. Even his shirt seemed to feel softer. "Better?"

"My head . . ." She shifted her hands to his neck, and he felt the ache being drawn toward where her fingers massaged him. He rolled his shoulders and sighed, feeling twenty pounds lighter. Tezza leaned forward and gave him a lingering peck on the cheek.

"See? I knew you weren't fine." She was moving away when he grabbed her wrist. He couldn't let her go; he never wanted to let her go. Not just because he loved her, not because she could ease his discomfort, but because everything was discomfort compared to her presence.

He looked up at her. "You still want to go to Descaret?"

Her eyes lit. She came around the couch to see him better, but her posture was guarded. "Don't tease."

"I'm not. I'm serious. Let's go."

"I'm sorry, what's happening over here?" Saint asked, and Sam turned to find them all staring at him, the game paused.

"We're getting married," Sam replied.

"Really?" Abbie squeaked, and he nodded. "Congratulations, you two!"

Edward came over, grinning, and shook his hand firmly before drawing Tezza into a side hug. "That's fantastic! Please let Ms. Scrope know your date as soon as possible, and I'll rearrange my schedule—"

"No, you misunderstand. We're getting married *tonight*. We're eloping."

Silence fell over the room. His friends' faces were contorted; Edward opened his mouth, then closed it, looking at Abbie, who was scowling. Saint, if Sam was reading him correctly, was livid, and Saint's date just looked uncomfortable.

"I'm getting better at nonverbals, but this," he said, gesturing in a circle toward them, "is mostly nonsense to me. Would somebody please say something?"

Saint stood, took a step forward, and opened his mouth, then froze suddenly. "Edward, did you get a cat?"

Sam's head snapped toward the door. There it was, the tortoiseshell, exactly as he'd seen it that first night, tail twitching lazily, standing just two feet inside the doorway, sniffing at the wire bookshelf that held board games and Ping-Pong paddles.

"Get it!" Sam shouted, but Tezza was ahead of him already, and he could feel her rallying the magic to her, quicker now. The animal darted toward the door, but Tezza threw out a spell to slam it shut just before it could go through, and even he could feel the magic send out a hard ripple when the pressure in the room changed.

"T, we've got to get the royals out of here," he said, creeping closer to the animal where it hid behind a bookshelf.

"No, I'm not opening the door, it'll get away. Whoever did this isn't very skilled or it would've walked right through the door. It's blunt magic; we're putting an end to it tonight."

The cat scrambled to avoid her and darted across the room, causing Saint's date to scream. *Honestly.*

The door swung open, and their weekend security counterparts stood there looking on full alert.

"Shut the door!" Sam and Tezza both yelled, and the men quickly complied.

"Your Majesties," Simonson directed, "get over by the door with Blake and Peterson. Everyone else, spread out and find the damn thing."

"All this fuss over a cat?" Abbie asked as Edward ushered her toward the door.

"It's not just a cat," Sam muttered as he circled the pool table.

"We've been seeing it in the hallways at night. It's some sort of magical apparition, and we've got to find out who's casting it. We defended the offices and the residence," Tezza said, distracted.

"But we apparently forgot about this room," said Sam.

"I didn't forget," Tezza muttered as she got on her hands and knees to look under the couch. "I was being strategic. It's not free, you know." A paw swiped her across the nose, and she cursed, holding her face. "Real claws, FYI."

"I'll flush it from the other side and you catch it," Sam said, grabbing a pool cue from the hanging rack on the wall.

She grimaced. "Fine, but I'm defending myself. That thing's not tearing me to shreds."

Sam slid the cue under the leather couch and he heard the animal hiss. He scooted the stick a little farther, and the cat darted out—into Tezza's waiting arms. She held it up triumphantly by the scruff of its neck as it swiped and hissed at her. The pounding on the game room door startled them so much, she almost dropped it.

Prince Simon stood in the doorway, his eyebrows drawn hard together, his mouth pulled down into an infuriated frown, his hands on his hips, his slightly bewildered security looming over him, panting.

"Give me my cat," he demanded, his chest heaving.

"*Your* cat?" Edward replied, staring at his youngest brother, perplexed, and Tezza smiled.

"Of course, Your Highness. Of course," she said, walking over to Simon and placing the frazzled creature in his arms. He stroked its head protectively, checking it for damage, then glowered at Macias. Sam felt something intangible in the room shift, and Tezza speared Simon with a disbelieving glare.

"No. You'd regret that," she said, her voice low. "Mind your manners, Your Highness."

Simon's eyes flashed with surprise before his head dropped.

"What in the world is going on?" Abbie asked, elbowing her way out of the protective circle her temporary security had created.

"Was he threatening you just now?" Edward's arms were crossed, his face hard. Tezza nodded once, and Simon suddenly shrank under the angry gaze of four adults who loved him.

"I'm sorry," he mumbled. "Mum can't have a real cat around . . ."

"Stand down, backup security," Peterson said into the radio. "Repeat, stand down. Threat neutralized."

Tezza turned to Abbie. "Grand Duchess, your brother-in-law has been playing with forces he doesn't understand. I suggest he start lessons with me this week until we can find him a better tutor."

His eyes shifted from upset to interested in a flash. "Will you teach me to make more animals?"

"A whole menagerie, Your Highness, but first, we'll work on boundaries . . ."

Remembering himself, Sam strode over to the wall and put away the cue as he grabbed the first aid kit. He caught Tezza by the elbow and led her over to the couch.

"Easy, petunia."

"I'm going to put Simon and his magical cat apparition back to bed," Edward said.

"I'll help," Abbie put in, ushering Simon out of the room, leaving Sam and Tezza with Saint and his date.

Sam sat on Tezza sideways and got out the antibiotic gel.

"Is this really necessary?" she griped.

"You're the worst patient in Orangiers."

"I am not," she shot back, turning her head away, defending herself lamely, swatting at his hands.

"Fine. Worst in the world, then," he said, chasing her with his slathered finger, trying not to let the goopy feeling of the gel bother him. "You're too tough for your own good." He caught her chin with his other hand and gingerly applied the medicine to the scratches the cat had left on her nose. "They're not deep, but this face is too pretty to scar. Your face is my favorite." He kissed her gently, then cleaned his fingers with a wipe. Sam felt Saint watching them, and he glanced at him out of the corner of his eye. *Arms crossed, gaze level, eyebrows neutral, mouth quirking. Assessing, but guarded . . . perhaps mildly amused? It's hard to tell with him. He looked really angry earlier . . .*

"So I'm going to take off," the woman whose name Sam couldn't remember muttered, giving Saint a peck on the cheek as she slung her purse over her shoulder.

"I'll call you," he said, not turning his attention from Sam and Tezza. As soon as she was out of the room, he pointed an accusatory finger at Sam.

"You're not eloping. Not tonight, not ever."

Sam cocked his head. "Why not? We're in love. Weddings are expensive and a pain to plan. What's the problem?"

Saint ran a hand through his hair, pulling at the ends of it, ruining his carefully gelled style. "What's the problem? Sam, you barely know each other. And she's literally just gotten out of a marriage. Yes, he'd been gone a long time, but it looks *bad*. It looks like you were just biding your time. And your families won't be there. And—and . . ." He trailed off as Edward and Abbie came back into the room, looking grave. "Help me out here, guys."

Edward shook his head. "You were doing fine. Keep going."

Saint huffed a sigh. "I know you're both hard-core and efficient, but you're going to be sorry you didn't have pictures and the dress and everything. You can't rush this."

Sam turned to Tezza. "He makes some sense."

"He does," she agreed. "I would like you to meet my family in person. Let's start with scheduling that trip if we can corral all my brothers." Sam let his face show how less than thrilled he felt, and she laughed. "I won't let them pound you, sugarlump."

"Sugarlump," Abbie whispered, grinning from ear to ear. "She called him 'sugarlump.' That's so wonderful. This is so wonderful!"

"So now that we're not eloping, we're back to wonderful?" Sam asked. His friends nodded, and he answered with his own nod. *I will never figure these people out.*

"Fine. But I'm not waiting more than three months," he said, "and you cannot wear black during the ceremony."

"Bad news."

He pulled away to see her face. "Oh?"

"Traditional Op'Ho'Lonian wedding dresses are always black, to symbolize how only death will part us."

Sam let out a deep sigh, shaking his head, and she laughed.

"I'll consider another color," Tezza replied. "Now get off, you're heavy."

He crossed his arms. Her nostrils flared. He followed her gaze to his biceps and snickered inwardly. *This woman is totally into me. That should scare me more than it does.*

"Make me."

"I could." She pushed at his chest halfheartedly.

"I know you can. So do it."

"I hate freeform," she growled, "and I *hate* having an audience."

Abbie snickered, then stopped when Tezza shot her a look.

"And I hate hand-to-hand. Do it."

Tezza glared at him, then closed her eyes, concentrating. He felt invisible hands grab him under the arms and lift him a few inches, then plop him on the couch next to her.

"You did it!" he cried, elated, taking her shoulders in his hands. "You couldn't do that when we met. I told you I'd help. You questioned my ability to assist in redeveloping your skills, but I found a method—several, actually—and you were wrong to doubt me. Say it. Say it out loud right now. Say you were wrong to doubt me, T. Fine, don't say it, I know it's true. And if we keep working at it, you'll continue to improve. You're already an invaluable asset to Edward and Abbie, but you can always get better."

Tezza was looking over his shoulder, and she almost looked . . . embarrassed? *Am I embarrassing her?* He twisted to see what she was looking at. Abbie had her head on Edward's chest and her arms around his waist. Edward had an arm around her shoulders, and Saint had one hand in his mussed hair again. They were all beaming at him.

"What are they doing?"

"Being happy for you, sugarlump."

"For us, you mean." He paused, and then she beamed, too. "This was stressful. I'd like to take you home now."

"That's the most I've ever heard him talk," Abbie whispered as he stood up, and he shook his head, laughing.

"I enjoy talking to Tezza."

"Mate, it was more like talking *at her* than talking to her," Saint drawled.

*Oh, really, Francis?* "Who's taking a woman home tonight?" Sam asked, not looking at Saint, holding out a hand to help Tezza off the deep couch cushions.

"Pardon?" Saint asked.

"Where's your date?" Sam asked. Tezza took his hand, smirking, and stood up.

"She left," he muttered.

Sam turned and looked him in the eye to better make his point. "Right. And mine's still right here, so I'll let you draw your own conclusions about who's better with women here."

He helped Tezza into her coat and they left hand in hand while his friends' mouths were still hanging open in shock, letting their laughter follow him down the hall.

# Epilogue

TEZZA LAY IN THE PITCH black of her bedroom. She'd pushed the heavy quilt off her husband's body and replaced it with her own weight. Under her head, Sam's chest rose and fell evenly, but she knew he was awake. He always woke before she did, even when he didn't have to go into the office at Travis and Simonson Weaponry. His arms came around her and squeezed her closer, and she rolled more on top of him.

"Hi."

"Hi," he replied, his eyes still closed. He rubbed her arm a little.

"Happy anniversary."

He smiled and opened one eye. "Happy anniversary."

"Did you forget?"

He scowled good-naturedly. "No."

"Did you get me a present?"

"Of course. I wouldn't repeat last year's disaster. I'm not stupid."

"A poem is nice, but a poem is not a present."

"Yes, so you said, and loudly."

"You're learning, though." She kissed his chest, and he jumped. "Give me a hint?"

He shook his head, staring down at her. She let her hands wander up and down his torso in firm, long strokes over his T-shirt and he grunted.

"Sam," she murmured, "I have a question for you."

"I'm listening, love."

"We've been married three years . . ."

"Yes."

"Do you think you'll ever get tired of . . ."

He placed his hands over hers to still them. "Of what?"

She slid up his body to whisper in his ear. "Do you think you'll ever get tired of . . . stealing my covers? I'm cold."

In a flash, she was on her back with her wrists pinned to the bed and her grinning husband hovering over her.

"Never, love. It's my secret weapon. I get more snuggling that way." He kissed her neck, nuzzling behind her ear. "Do you think you'll ever get tired of messing with me?"

"Never, sugarlump," she breathed, as she tried to wriggle her hands free of his grip. "I will mess with you forever."

"Well, that's settled, then," he said, lowering his body to hers. "You know, sometimes, on a special date . . ."

"Like an anniversary?" she asked, smiling against his scratchy cheek.

"Yes," he murmured, kissing along her jaw. "On a special date, like an anniversary, couples like to do a certain special activity together . . . It's early yet, but I was thinking we could—"

"Mami?" A small voice came through the closed door, and Sam's forehead fell to her shoulder, his warm breath heavy on her neck.

"Don't answer yet," he whispered. "Maybe she'll go back to bed . . ."

A hesitant knock. "Mami? I kind of had an accident last night. I need new sheets."

With a sigh, Sam released Tezza's arms and flopped onto his back. "Come in, love," he called. The girl opened the door and peered into the darkness.

"And I'm hungry. Are we having breakfast soon?"

"You're only hungry because you didn't eat your supper last night, monkey," Sam chided gently. "You used to *like* macaroni and cheese! Why won't you eat it when Dad makes it?"

"You didn't put hot dogs in it," Tezza said as she pulled on her robe. "That's how her foster mama did it. We told you that."

He threw his hands in the air. "Hot dogs are disgusting, the texture is repulsive!"

"Disgusting to you is delicious to her . . ."

"You'd think in six years on this earth she'd have learned to have better taste," he grumbled.

"You tell her, Dad." Tezza went to the door to greet their daughter. "Good morning, Raquel." She pressed the girl's head against her belly in a hug and smoothed her long dark hair.

"Good morning, Mami. I want waffles with Yaya's sauce on them."

"Oh, me too," Sam piped up behind her, and she smiled. "And T?"

"Mmm?"

"I still want to do that special activity we were discussing, later . . ."

She glanced at him over her shoulder, giving him a wink their daughter wouldn't see. "I don't see how it's *special* if we did it yesterday . . ." She sighed as if pained. "But if you insist."

"I do, T." He grinned. "I do."

### Thank you for reading my book!

Want to see what happens when Sam went Groom-zilla and threatened to call it all off? Why did he agree to a beach wedding, anyway? You can grab this free bonus scene *Sand and Secret Messages: An Almost-Widow Wedding* when you sign up for my newsletter, The West Wind. Find a screen and follow this link now: BookHip.com/ZNMRFL [1]

---

**MORE BOOKS FROM FIONA WEST**
**The Borderline Chronicles**
*The Ex-Princess*, Abbie and Edward (Book 1)
*The Un-Queen*, Abbie and Edward (Book 2)
*The Jinxed Journalist*, Saint and Brooke (Book 3)
*The Semi-Royal*, Rhodie and Arron (Book 4), coming February 2020

## ACKNOWLEDGEMENTS

- With gratitude to my sweet family, my inspiration in so many ways.
- Thanks to Sylvia Cottrell, my amazing editor. Don't think you're off the hook just because your family needs you...I've got dibs when you start working again.
- Thanks to Steven Novak, my awesome cover artist. You nailed this one.
- Thanks to my writing group, Ruth and Magalie. Your conversations and insights keep my creative juices flowing! (Is that weird? That's probably weird.)
- Thanks to my critique partner, Angela Boord, and my beta readers, Cora, Laura, and Christine. Your help is invaluable! I wish I had some way to repay your kindness...other than free books, of course.
- Thanks to my sensitivity reader, Alisha Anderson with Salt and Sage Books. Your professional insights into the piece have really elevated it and made it something special. I appreciate you!

# Connect with Fiona!

Thanks so much for taking the time to read my work. I hope you enjoyed reading it even more than I enjoyed writing it, though I doubt that's possible. Being an author is a dream come true, and getting to share my books with delightful, thoughtful readers like you just adds to the sweetness. Drop me a line and let me know what you thought or leave a review on Amazon or Goodreads!

Sign up for my monthly newsletter, The West Wind, for freebies, deleted scenes, book reviews, and insight into my writing process.

On Twitter as @FionaWestAuthor

On Facebook as @authorfionawest

On Instagram as @fionawestauthor

On Goodreads as Fiona West

Or email me at fiona@fionawest.net. I love talking to fans!